WICKED HEX

THE ROYALS: WITCH COURT BOOK 3

MEGAN MONTERO

LEO PRESS

For Grandpa, 90 and still rocking out!
Xoxo-Megan

The Royals: Witch Court Season 1

Wicked Trials- FREE when you join my newsletter

Wicked Witch

Wicked Magic

Wicked Hex

Wicked Potion

Wicked Queen

The Royals: Warlock Court Season 2

Wicked Omen- Coming Fall 2019

CHAPTER 1

ALATRIS

I folded my hands behind my back while I looked up at the sky for long moments after my eldest daughter, Zinnia, flew off with my dragon. With each inhalation I took, the haze of madness ebbed away. I stood sucking in deep breaths of the damp air until I could get past the rage. *How could they not see I was doing this for all of the witch and warlock kind? Our society would be better if they just LISTENED to me! Deep breath in, deep breath out.* At least I had her, flesh of my flesh, blood of my blood. A slow smile spread over my face. The power she wielded was so similar to my own, but so much more. I stood there until the ice mess the dragon made melted into one big puddle that seeped into my shoes.

Dario Malback, a warlock from one of the oldest

magical families in Evermore, walked out to stand beside me. "They've taken the dragon."

I rolled my eyes. "Obviously."

"And this displeases you?" He turned his head to the side, looking me up and down with his gold eyes that sparkled like coins. His face was covered in the kind of wrinkles only an extensive life full of scowls could make. Long black hair fell back from the widow's peak on his forehead all the way down to the middle of his back. He pressed his thin lips into a hard line, waiting for my next word. Dario and I had spent centuries together. Experience alone demanded his silence while he waited for my reply.

"On the contrary, I am very pleased." All around me, those subjects loyal to my cause, the right cause, fell to their knees, filled with unfamiliar power she'd forced upon them. *What an intriguing notion.* Rather than killing the men I sent to stop her, she punished them . . . cruelly.

Perhaps the apple doesn't fall far from the rotting tree, after all. I spun on my heels and began walking back toward my castle. My patience was so very close to snapping. I could feel the churning eruption building in my chest. It scorched hotter with each passing moment. At times, I feared the rage would overtake me and never let me go. But now that she was here, my Zinnia, things could be different. She could be my . . . heir. My one true heir. The sound of footsteps drew me from my thoughts.

Is someone behind me? I gathered my magic in the palm of my hand, ready to kill anyone who dared challenge me. Dario caught up to me and met my stride. I gave him a sideways glance. "You're still with me?"

"I never left, sire." His brow furrowed, and he narrowed his eyes at me.

Does he think I'm going mad too?

He cleared his throat. "Perhaps you could switch the men's powers back to the body they belong in?"

"Hmm . . . tell me, why would I do such a thing?" I glanced over my shoulder at where they ran around in hysterical circles, hitting each other with energy balls and some of them self-destructing.

"I would think—"

I stopped dead and faced him. "That is your problem, Dario. You needn't be the one to think." I motioned toward the men behind us. "What purpose would it serve me to have others who couldn't stop her from taking what's mine? Furthermore, they are weak, and I've no room for weakness among my ranks." *My blackouts are enough.*

Dario bowed his head. "Yes, sire."

"Yes indeed." I strode toward the castle once more,

following the winding cobblestone path up toward the thick walls laid with stone surrounding it. At the corner of each wall stood a turret. Each one was manned by a loyal follower ready to give their life for me. The oversized wooden door slid up into the wall. The clanking of metal chains and turning of gears sounded as it rose inch by inch and stopped only high enough for me to walk through. Three strides and I was within my castle walls. Silence greeted me, and I relished every moment of it. At the town center, I stopped again, noting how not even the horses made a sound when I was near. They'd been trained well. "We'll have to strengthen our enchantments on the island. Now that Zinnia has blood ties here, there will be no stopping her if she gets back. See it done."

Dario's eyebrows rose to his hairline, his jaw dropped, and he pressed his hand to his chest. "Me, sire?"

"No, the other idiot standing next to me!" I threw my arms up in the air. Blackness swarmed the sides of my vision as I leaned over him, gathering my magic in my hands once more. "Must . . . I . . . spell . . . everything . . . out?"

Dario took a small step back yet didn't flinch away from me. "No, sire. I will strengthen the enchantments within the hour."

4

Breath in, breath out, rein it in. The black dots receded from my vision. I let the magic seep back into my body where it lay waiting for the time I would strike out. I tugged at the sleeves of my jacket and brushed my hands down my black dress pants. "Very well, but first you will accompany me to the throne room."

"As you wish." He bowed at the waist and swept his arm to the side, indicating I should lead the way.

Will he stab me in the back the moment I turn it? I pressed my finger to my lips. "After you, my friend." I waved him forward. If anyone was going to be stabbed in the back, it would be him.

Dario didn't hesitate to move. He simply straightened his stance and walked through the town square into the tunnel that led into the main castle. All the while I stared at the back of his head, wondering if my long-time follower plotted against me or if I could trust his loyalty. All of this drew me to one final conclusion. I needed an heir to carry my name on, to trust. *Though my own father shouldn't have trusted me.* I waved the thought away, knowing this time would be different.

After traversing the stone spiral staircase that led to my throne room, I waited for Dario to unlock the steel door. Very few people knew about this entrance, yet it was the way I used each time I came here. The door hinges creaked open as Dario held it wide-open for me. I brushed the heavy tapestry to the side and swept into the room. The smell of damp cobblestone hung in the air. Outside, the temperature was warm and humid, as all tropical islands would be, but within the walls of the castle it dropped at least fifteen degrees. At times, it seeped into my skin, chilling me to the bone.

As I strode into my throne room, Catherine, my prisoner, jumped to her feet. My younger daughter, Ophelia, remained on the floor where she'd been sitting beside her. *Plotting. They're always plotting against me.* Black dots swarmed the sides of my vision as I surged toward her. Ophelia, the daughter who was supposed to be loyal, spent more and more of her time at my prisoner's side. "You think to plot against me?"

Ophelia's eyes rounded into coal-colored saucers. She rose to her feet and took a step back and held her hand out. "I would never, Father."

I lifted my hand across my body and snapped it forward, cracking her in the cheek. The skin on the back of my hand stung from the smack. Her head snapped back, and those long black braids whipped around. When I raised my hand for the next blow, she threw her shoulders back and met my gaze. All life drained from her features. She gave me that black dead look she'd mastered when she was four. Fury raged from my chest out to my fingers. My body quaked from head to toe. "You will be loyal to me! Do you hear me, girl?"

I pulled my hand back farther, about to turn her other cheek as red as I had the first. Before I could land the blow, pain exploded across the side of my face. I stumbled back, clutching my face. "Who dare—"

"You want to hit someone? Let's go, a-hole." Catherine leapt in front of Ophelia and held her fists up. An angry red welt marred the side of her own face.

I brushed the back of my fingers over my cheek. "Ah, we both know anything I do to you I'll feel it myself." I held my wrist up and flashed her the mark that was the bane of my existence. Oh, how I loved and hated her. "Soul mates, my love."

Catherine's lips tilted into a frown as she glowered at me. "I wish I'd never completed the bonding with you."

Pang! What little feelings I had left were stung. "Ha! But you did."

She rolled her eyes. "I didn't even know it was you! You lying, cheating snake. A glamour! You held a glamour up for months, deceitful bastard."

She launched herself at me. The chains around her wrists rattled as she moved. One moment she stood before me, and the next she hauled her leg back and let her knee connect with my crotch. The wind left my lungs, and pain ran up from my groin to my shoulders.

My knees buckled, and I fell to the ground, cupping myself.

"Catherine, don't!" Ophelia cried out.

I let a slow smile spread across my lips. "Hurts, doesn't it?"

Catherine hunched over, sucking in deep breaths and clutching her lower stomach. "I don't care!" She threw her hands out, and her magical golden sparks gathered in her palms.

Ophelia rushed at her back and wrapped her arms around Catherine's torso. "Stop. You'll only make it worse for yourself."

Dario stepped out in between us. He threw his shoulders back and looked up at the ceiling. When he turned, he met my gaze for the barest of moments before holding both his hands out as if he held two stop signs. "Need I remind you both we've done this before and neither of you faired for the better?"

"Tell him to keep his hands to himself and I promise I'll do the same." Though she spoke through clenched teeth, I continued to be drawn to her plump lips.

"Is this agreeable to you, sire?" He turned toward me with his eyebrows raised.

I spun on my heels and walked up the three steps leading toward my throne. "Parenting is never easy."

"Is that what you call it?" Catherine snapped. "You have no right to be a parent to anyone . . . ever."

I dropped into the chair, and the cushion dipped beneath me as I slouched back into the chair. The anger I'd felt only a moment ago gave way to that stinging hurt that only she could inflict upon me. "Says the woman who kept my daughter away from me for sixteen years."

"Precisely." She crossed her arms over her chest.

Long ago I'd once seen a movie where a large blob-like creature chained a beautiful maiden to his own throne. I always thought it a brilliant idea. Though Catherine burned the two-piece dress I'd given her, she remained defiant and stayed in the beat-up jeans and black sweater she'd been wearing the day I took her. Her wild chocolate waves were tied into a knot on the top of her head. When she looked at me with those sapphire eyes, the same eyes our daughter had, my anger flared once more. "I can't believe you kept her from me."

"Wait a second." Ophelia glanced from me to Catherine and back again. "I have a sister?"

Catherine narrowed her eyes at me before answering, "Half sister, yes."

My emotionless, coldhearted, calculating daughter's mouth dropped wide-open. "How come you never told me?"

I shrugged and waved her comment away. "Didn't seem important at the time."

"Not important! This changes eve—"

"This changes nothing!" I jumped to my feet. "The only thing it changes is who will become my heir."

Ophelia took a small step back. "I am your heir."

"Perhaps." I shrugged and glanced down at Catherine. Her cheeks turned bright red.

"Zinnia will never be the heir to your empire. Never."

I ran my fingers over my jawline. "Are you so sure about that?"

Catherine held her chin up. "Without question."

"I've already taken her mother." I dropped back into the throne and began to study my nails. "Let's see how righteous she feels when I take the rest."

"She will never be like you." She shook her head back and forth.

"Oh, but, my dear, she already is." I held my hand up and let the sparkling magic gather in my palm. My eyes were affixed to the glittering swirl of energy. "Dario."

"Yes, sire?" He moved to the center of my court.

"I believe your son is about Zinnia's age?"

Dario glanced around the room. "He is seventeen."

"Then I do believe it's time for him to go to school." I turned from the ball in my hand toward Dario.

"He attends private lessons, sire."

I kicked the footrest at my feet down the steps. The golden block-like piece skidded to a halt at Dario's feet. "And I'm telling you he will attend Evermore Academy now. The Fallen cannot turn him away, and I believe it's time to get a man on the inside."

"As you wish." Dario inclined his head. "I will make arrangements today."

"Ophelia dear, don't you think we need a man on the inside?" My words seemed to draw her out of whatever shocked stupor she was in.

The angry red welt still marred her pale cheek, yet she straightened her shoulders and gave me the cold look I'd grown so accustomed to. "Yes, Father."

"It doesn't matter what you do or who you send after her. Zinnia will forever and always do what she thinks is right." Catherine yanked at the chain around her wrist, and I felt the pinching of her skin on my own arm.

I rubbed at my wrist. "Oh, my dear, I'm counting on it."

CHAPTER 2

"Somebody help me!" I screamed so loud the words scratched up my throat. Lights flickered on one by one, illuminating the courtyard. Each lamp chased away the shadows around me. I cradled Tuck's head in my lap. A cold sweat broke out over his body, and his eyes had yet to open. His auburn hair drifted back from his face in a tattered mess. "Niche! I need you."

The veins in his arms and neck turned to a dark black that I could see through his pale skin, as though I could see the magic Alataris used against him slowly spreading through his body. The wicked phoenix tattoo on his neck pulsed an angry burning red, as though it too was trying to fight whatever Alataris had done to him. I pressed my finger to it, then yanked it back, shaking out the stinging burn. The mark around my wrist felt as though it were tied tighter than ever before cutting off the circulation and making my fingers numb and tingling. Everything in my body shifted, and a sudden sense of dread filled me. The two of us had steadily been getting closer and closer. I could feel him, his turmoil, everything he felt. Was it the soul mate bond I suspected he was going to tell me about? Or was it just my magic growing? I didn't know.

All at once, the muscles in his body tensed and he began seizing in my arms. "Oh, God. Tuck, hold on, just hold on."

I gently let his head fall to the ground and scrambled to get next to him and turn him on his side. I'd once took a first aid class and knew that when a person seized, they could choke. Hot tears ran down my cheeks, and my hands shook as I pressed them to his back and held him there while he shook. His eyes rolled in his head as I leaned over him, holding him until the tremors stopped. I whispered in his ear, "Don't die, Tuck. Please don't."

I rocked back and forth, feeling each and every tremor as if it were my own until the very last one shuddered through him. An eased breath drifted through his lips, and his body went limp in my arms. "No!"

My heart hammered in my chest, and my breaths came in panicked puffs. I wanted to ugly cry, the kind of cry that burned its way up my throat. The kind that left me gasping for air but was too lost to rein it in. The kind that made my whole body tremble and my bones rattle together. The kind I'd feel days later.

This wasn't some movie with a happily ever after. This was my life, and my happily ever after was lying at my feet fighting to breathe. Instead, I held it in, only letting the barest tears stream down my face. I swallowed around the ball in my throat and focused all my attention on him.

"What the hell is going on here?"

I snapped my head up and met his eye. Matteaus stood above me with his hands crossed over his chest. At this time of night, the headmaster of Evermore Academy looked like an angel of death rather than one of the Fallen, the immortal species that ruled not only the academy but the world of Evermore. Strands of his multicolored hair fell across the sharp planes of his face, and his ocean-blue eyes were narrowed into tiny slits at me.

"He's dying." I swiped at my tears with the back of my hand. I could barely speak the words I knew were true. The second they left my lips, the world spun, and I clung even harder to Tuck. This couldn't be the end of our story. Not now. It was too soon. We didn't even get the chance to be more . . . to do more together. A light sob escaped my lips. I pressed them together harder to hold it in.

"He's not dying. Not on my watch." Though Tucker was six-three and at least two hundred and fifty pounds, Matteaus scooped him up into his arms as though he weighed nothing.

Niche came running out into the courtyard. Her fire engine red hair streamed out behind her. The lab coat I'd grown so used to seeing her in billowed out from her body with each step she took. When she got to us, her hands fluttered over Tuck, her eyes turned into round saucers behind the thick rims of her black glasses. "What happened?"

"I-I don't know. W-we freed the dragon and she returned back to Alaska, but A-Alataris was there and they faced off. He did something to him. I don't know." My body shook from head to toe. Cold fear coursed through me. *Please don't die. Please don't die.* Boom, boom, boom echoed around the courtyard.

"What in the actual fu—heck is that?" Matteaus turned his head around, looking for the source of what sounded like a battering ram against a castle door. *Whack!* The noise grew louder, until a door on the other side of the courtyard exploded inward, sending shards of wood flying in all directions. A feral growl came from the corner of the courtyard, where two piercing violet eyes glowed in the darkness.

Matteaus slowly turned away from the creature and whispered, "Run. Just run for that door." He pointed down the long hall where the dorm rooms were, and that thick wooden door sat at the very end.

I didn't know what it was, but it was the size of a small horse and I didn't want to wait around to find out. I turned and followed right behind him. Tucker bounced in his arms as Niche kept pace beside him. When I glanced back, I stopped dead and spun on my heels.

Matteaus yelled over his shoulder. "You got a death wish?"

"No." I shook my head and faced off against Kumi, the wolf-like creature that haunted one of the rooms in Evermore Academy. The ground rumbled under my feet as she charged out toward me. Her thick midnight fur would've blended in with the dark sky if it weren't for the streaks of ocean-blue fur that marked her chest, down her legs, and the tip of each of her nine tails. I held my hand up. "Stop!"

Kumi slid to a halt like a dog on a hardwood floor. Her paws spun trying to gain traction and her body tilted sideways until she smacked into the ground and ended up lying at my feet. When she looked up at me with those wide eyes, I bent over and ran my fingers through her fur just under her ear. My panic ebbed, and the shaking in my body eased. "What are you doing?"

You needed me.

I froze. "Did you just talk to me?"

Did you just hear me in your head?

We both shared a "holy crap" look. Niche came to my side. "We have to get Tuck to the infirmary."

Though I wanted to understand what was happening between Kumi and me, Tucker was way more important. I nodded and followed behind her, only to hear those heavy footfalls trailing close by. I wanted to stop and tell her she couldn't come along, but right now I could only focus on one thing at a time.

Matteaus led us down the hall where some of the dorm rooms were. Doors opened as the students popped their heads out, their brows furrowed as they took in Tucker's limp body. Then their eyes widened, and they slammed their doors as Kumi stomped down the hallway behind us.

"She can't come with us." Niche pressed her hand to Tucker's head, brushing away some of the sweat.

I can, and I will. Kumi's words brushed through my mind so effortlessly, as though we'd been communicating this way all along.

I shook my head. "Nothing I can do about that right

this second." My only concern was for Tuck, so if a mythological creature was hell-bent on coming along with us, then so be it.

Once we reached the end of the hall, there was a thick wooden door. Matteaus leaned back on one foot and with the other he kicked it wide-open. The hefty black wings on his back pulsed and moved. Black feathers fell to the ground as he took the stairs two at a time. I hurried behind him, pumping my arms to keep up. Kumi shoved her big body through the door, splintering the doorframe.

Once we reached the top floor, Matteaus turned down a short hall and pushed through the double doors leading into the infirmary. Two identical rows of cots lined the walls on either side of the room. At the end of the aisle sat a bald-headed man with large tortoise-shell glasses perched on the end of his narrow nose. When he rose from behind his desk, his long purple robes fluttered. He raced around and pointed to the cot nearest to him. "Put him here."

Matteaus laid him out over the white linen. Tuck fell back on the cot like a limp fish. His skin was ashen. His black shirt clung to his sweat-covered body. The doctor leaned over him and lifted his eyelid, then he snapped his fingers and a small pen light appeared. He shined it into Tucker's eyes and gave a low grunt.

"What's that mean? Is he going to be okay?" I stepped closer to the bed, but Matteaus clamped a hand down on my shoulder, stopping me from getting any closer. Before I could shrug his grip off, he dropped his hand.

The doctor didn't answer my question. He simply turned toward me and pushed his glasses back up his nose. "What was done to him?"

"I-I'm not sure." Memories of Alataris holding him up by his neck and that black smoke billowing from his lips and seeping into Tuck's mouth, eyes, and nose assailed me. I curled my hands into fists. Alataris was now on my shit list. It didn't matter what it took, he was going down. Not just for me, but for what he did to Tuck, my mom, and all of Evermore.

The door to the infirmary flew open, and the rest of our crew flooded in like a menacing tide, with Brax, our hulking tiger shifter, in the front. It was the first time I'd seen him in anything different than a black tank top and black and gray army fatigues. Yet there he stood in a huge baggy sweatshirt and sweatpants to match. He ran his hand over his crew cut blond hair. "What happened?" His Russian accent was so thick I could barely make out his words.

Before I could answer him, Kumi spun around and took up a defensive position in front of us. With her paws spread wide, she lowered her head and bared her teeth at them. A low growl rumbled deep in her chest. Kumiho was a mythological beast who until recently was held within a secured room at Evermore Academy. I'd stumbled into her room a few days ago and felt connected to her ever since. To me she was more like an oversized wolf with nine tails. To everyone else she was a legendary creature who reaped souls for fun. At least that's what the rumors said. Personally I didn't believe them.

Brax held his arms out, stopping the others from passing him. He too bared his teeth, letting them elongate into sharp tiger points, and hissed in her direction. When he pushed his sleeves up, tiger stripes appeared across his skin.

Grayson too stepped up and let his vamp fangs slide down. "Best step aside, puppy, or I'll be taking a chunk out of you."

"Not before I send her back to where she came from." Beckett was ready on the other side of Brax with a ball of magic waiting to be tossed in the palm of his hand. His blond hair was sticking out in different directions and falling into his eyes, as though he'd been tossing and turning in his sleep. Dark circles hung under his teal eyes.

"Stop," I snapped. Everyone froze in place, including Kumi. *Let them pass.*

She dropped down on her haunches with a moan. *I don't like the one with the fangs.*

Two of them have fangs . . .

She glanced up at me with those bright violet eyes. *Then I don't like either of them.*

I glanced from Tuck at our group coming in and back again. "We freed the dragon, and Alataris was there waiting for us."

Grayson eyed Kumi as he raced around Brax and past the doctor to stand next to Tuck's head. He too reached down and pulled one of his eyelids back. "His pupils are fixed and dilated." He reached down and pressed two of his fingers to the inside of Tucker's wrist. "Pulse is faint at best, love."

My heart sank into my stomach. "What does that mean?"

"It means he's . . . well, he's . . . dying." Grayson motioned over Tuck's body. "His injuries are extensive."

Extensive. I wanted to vomit on the floor. This couldn't be happening.

The doctor elbowed him aside. "Mr. Shade, will you desist doing my job and move out of the way?"

Grayson held his hands up and took a step back, letting the doctor get closer to Tuck once again. Normally, Grayson wore pressed black pants and a button-down shirt. But now standing before me this late at night, he wore striped navy pajama pants and a long-sleeved white thermal shirt. The rest of the crew gathered around Tuck's bed in a semi-circle, each of them in their pajamas. I didn't know it'd be so late when we got back. Hell, I didn't even know what day it was.

Niche stepped in front of me. "You need to tell me what you saw, exactly what you saw."

I nodded. "Alataris, he . . . he wrapped his hand around Tuck's neck and lifted him off the ground. Then he looked like he was whispering something in his ear. Black smoke came out of his mouth and seeped into Tuck." I pressed my hand over my throat. "Into his mouth, eyes, and nose. I've never seen anything like it."

Niche's face paled, and she took a step back. She pressed her fingers to her lips. "A hex . . ."

Her eyes widened, and she began running around the infirmary, opening cabinets and pulling out different colored stones and candles. I rushed to her side. "What can I do to help?"

Nova ran up and took the stones from Niche's hand. "I'll place them." Her white-blond hair was tied in a high knot on the top of her head, and her satin pajamas hung loose from her body. "Come on, Zinnia. We have to work fast."

I held my hands out, gathering up whatever crystals Niche gave to me. Serrina, our Queen of Desires, started collecting candles in her hands and carrying them to line them up on the windowsill. Even this late at night, her streaked blond hair looked like she'd just stepped out of a salon. As she placed each candle one by one so carefully, I wanted to yell for her to hurry up, but she took her time. Niche's face paled as drops of sweat ran down her cheeks. She ran to another cabinet and pulled a bottle of oil from it. She lifted her hand and snapped her fingers.

Professor Davis appeared in the cot next to Tuck's. She had her quilt pulled up to her chin, and a soft snore drifted from her lips. Her fuzzy salt and pepper hair stuck out in tufts from under her brown velvet sleeping cap. A pitch-black cat snoozed over her legs. The cat's nose twitched as it sucked in deep breaths, sniffing. Its eyes drifted open ever so slightly, glimpsing at Kumi lying not even ten feet away. With a start, the cat blasted straight up into the air with a hiss. Its hair stuck out in all directions. It landed on Professor Davis' shoulder, who then sat straight up in bed. "Ah, what in the hell . . .?"

She looked around in all different directions. Her brown eyes were wide with shock. "What . . . where am I?"

Niche didn't waste time. "Infirmary. Need your help. Tuck has been hexed."

She threw the covers back and pulled the sleeves of her brown sleeping gown up. "I've said it before, I don't like being summoned like that, Niche." Her gaze landed on Tuck. "But for this, I'll forgive you."

Tabi, Queen of Elements, stepped forward and sent golden sparks from the tips of her fingers. "Fire!"

The candles sitting around Tuck sparked to life, sending the flames a few feet up into the air before they settled into a light flickering. The glowing light seemed to shimmer over Tabi's wild black curls. When her hazel eyes met mine, I saw she too was in panic mode. We all were. Tuck was our leader, the one who was the picture of good within our group.

Niche waved us all forward. "Every witch in this room needs to make a circle, hold hands . . ." She glanced over my shoulder. "Adrienne, you too. We're going to need all the power we can get."

Adrienne wasn't a witch or even a queen witch, but Niche believed she could fill in for our fifth queen to help stop Alataris. Her powers were sparse at best, but I agreed with Niche, we needed all we could get. Adrienne's tongue darted over her lips, and she looked at me with wide ebony eyes that matched her skin perfectly. When I held my hand out to her, she tossed her hip-length braids over her shoulder and moved past the line of knights watching us. Brax and Beckett stood ten feet from Kumi with their eyes locked on her.

Grayson took up a stance at the foot of Tuck's bed, staring down at him. "Don't like to see our roles reversed."

Though Grayson was the joker of our group with his dry British humor, there was no humor in his grave eyes now. He was right to worry. I could feel the pain and turmoil rolling through Tuck's body. It sank into my stomach, making me nauseous. I pressed the back of my hand to my mouth to stifle my gagging. I wanted to climb into bed next to him, to wrap my arms around his body and hold him close. But I couldn't. I stood between Adrienne and Tabi, holding their hands tighter than I should. But they didn't protest. The doctor and Professor Davis took up positions on either side of Niche. Matteaus stood farther back with his arms crossed over his chest. Though his face didn't show much, I could tell by the ticking in his jaw and the pulsing in his wings that he was concerned. His ocean eyes were locked on Tuck as if he was willing him to get better.

Niche squared her shoulders. "We have to try to remove the hex from Tuck, or at least ease it."

"Wait a second . . . just ease it?" I shifted from one foot to the other. "We need to break this now."

"We'll do our best." Niche met each of our eyes. "We're all going to need to do this. Open your powers up and let them flow through each other. Zinnia, focus everything you can on him, okay? And everyone repeat after me."

I nodded and turned my gaze on Tuck. "Okay, I can do this." *I will do this.*

Professor Davis cleared her throat. "Do your best, ladies. The hex has taken root. It will require a great deal of power."

Taken root? I sucked in a deep breath and waited for Niche to speak the words.

"Black as night remove this hex from my sight. Black as night remove this hex from my sight." When she looked at us, we all began chanting the words over and over again until they blurred together in a symphony of whispers. One syllable blended into the next, and I could feel our powers rising together.

My eyes widened when all our magic started streaming from our bodies. Golden ribbons flew from Tabi, purple streams flowed from Nova, red sparks flew from Serrina, and even my silver glittering magic. They gathered in a tornado of color above Tucker's body. I didn't break the circle or stop whispering the words, but I was transfixed by the power before me. As the queens of each of the five magical castes, we were the most powerful of all the witches in Evermore. Would it be enough to save Tuck?

Our powers curled together and fired into his chest. Tuck's body bowed off the cot, his arms flailed, and his mouth opened in a silent scream. I took a step forward. "Tuck!"

"Don't break the circle!" Niche bellowed.

I stepped back. Tabi squeezed my hand, holding me in place. I swallowed down my panic and kept on chanting. "Black as night remove this hex from my sight."

His body lifted up off the bed, hovering two feet off it. Our powers circled around him, illuminating him in a glowing array of colors. Black drops of sweat rose to the surface of his skin and drifted away from his body, each of them floating in mid-air.

"Professor Davis, the basin," Niche warned.

Professor Davis didn't move or hesitate. A copper bowl appeared on the floor at the foot of Tuck's bed. One by one, every drop of black sweat that came from his skin flew toward the bowl, gathering there. Bright light erupted from Tuck, blinding us all. Tabi's and Adrienne's hands fell from mine as I ducked my head and closed my eyes.

Then there was nothing but silence. I stood straight and blinked away the dots swarming my vision. Tuck drifted back down to the bed. His veins were no longer black, and the color returned to his cheeks.

The others looked as though they were about to collapse. Tabi leaned on Nova. Each of them was hunched over and breathing heavily. Serrina stumbled back and plopped onto the cot behind her. Even Niche and Professor Davis moved away from the rest of us at a slower pace. Each of them sat down at the first empty spot they could find.

Exhaustion like I'd never felt before pulled at me. My eyelids felt heavy and began to close all on their own. Even so, I pulled the cot behind me closer to his bed and sat down. "Why isn't he waking up?"

"Give it time. We'll just have to wait and see if it worked." Niche lumbered toward me, then patted my shoulder.

I'd never seen them all so drained before. They'd given everything they had to save Tuck. As I sat there on the cot next to his, I took his hand in mine and stared at his face, waiting for his eyes to open. We'd given everything we had.

I could only hope it was enough to save him.

CHAPTER 3

ZINNIA

It wasn't enough.

The veil of hazy sleep I was under had barely lifted when a wave of cold fear hit me so hard I shot straight up in the cot. The drops of sweat that'd gathered on my chest ran under my shirt and down my stomach. I sucked in a deep breath and brushed my wild locks back from my face. A pained whimper drew my gaze down toward Tucker. His eyes darted behind his lids, and the muscles in his body were twitching with tension. Only a fraction of color had returned to his face after we'd tried to remove the hex. His black shirt was soaked and clinging to him.

I reached out and smoothed the strands of hair back from his face. "Tuck? Tuck, you've got to wake up."

"Not sure that's going to happen." Matteaus' deep voice broke the hushed silence of the infirmary.

I yanked my hand away from Tuck's forehead. "Why do you say that?"

"If he was going to get better, I think it would've happened by now." He arched his eyebrow, then leaned in and whispered, "Something should be done about that."

"Like what?" I lowered my voice to match his. "We've done all we can."

"According to whom? If it were up to me, who was about to lose someone *dear* to me, I would do whatever it took." He pointedly looked at my wrist. Though I wore a bracelet to hide the soul mate mark, I felt like he was examining it. The mark, a thin line of connected infinity marks with tiny silvery pearls in between each one, surrounded my wrist. I'd been hiding it since it first appeared. But looking at Matteaus now, I wondered if he somehow knew.

I tugged at the thin sheet covering my legs. "How come you can't do whatever it takes now?"

Matteaus sighed. "I wish I could. The Creator knows I want to. But unless I'm ordered to, my hands are tied. Something about if I do it for you then how will you ever learn."

"This isn't like teaching someone how to cook. We're talking life or death here." I motioned to Tuck. "He is . . ." My breath hitched, and I cleared my throat. "Dying."

"But he won't, not if you do your research." He made a show of looking me up and down. "And perhaps get cleaned up. You look like you just fought a dragon."

I pursed my lips and gave him a sour look. "Helpful, very helpful."

"I've already said enough. Do your research and you'll know exactly what you need." Matteaus gave me a little salute, then began walking toward the double doors. The doctor stopped him on his way out, and they murmured to each other, all the while glancing back toward the cot where Tuck lay.

When I turned back toward him, his hands were curled into fists while he ground his teeth together. I smoothed my hand down his cheek. "What's going on behind those eyes of yours?"

Just then, his shoulders lifted up off the bed as he forced his head back. A pained moan escaped his clenched teeth. I rose from the cot I'd passed out on last night and shoved it back into place. Then I turned and sat next to Tuck. "I'll fix this. I promise."

"How's he doing, love?" Grayson strolled down the aisle, looking fresh from a shower. His dark mahogany hair was brushed back from his face. I'd never noticed it before, but in the bright sterile infirmary I saw flecks of crimson in his chocolate eyes. He straightened the sleeves of his button-down shirt and smoothed his hand over his black dress pants.

"How's he look like he's doing?" I snapped. How was he so calm, taking the time to be showered and dressed like it was any other day?

"Hey, calm down there. I've come to relieve you, so you can get a shower and maybe some rest." He looked me up and down. "You need it."

I rose to my feet and threw the sheet back down on the bed. "I'm tired of everyone telling me I look like hell when there are more important things to worry about."

Grayson held up his hands in surrender. "Are you saying you don't want to be my fake girlfriend anymore?"

"Ugh." I wanted to slap him so hard he'd feel it in his baby fangs. "I didn't want to be your fake anything to begin with."

"Zinnia, you need to calm down and think. This one option might not have worked completely, but it has bought us some time." He put his hands on his hips and looked down at Tuck. "Right now, everyone needs to be at their best, so if that means you get a shower and sleep for an hour, so be it."

I froze and held my hand up to silence him. "What did you just say?"

"You need a shower?" He shifted from one foot to the other and looked at me like I had six heads.

"No, the other part." I sucked in a breath. "There are other options. There have to be." I glanced down at Tuck, then back up at Grayson. "If anything changes, you come and get me right away, okay?"

I hurried toward the door. Grayson called after me, "Where are you going?"

"Shower, then to the library," I called over my shoulder.

"Keyword shower first, love," he muttered.

HALF AN HOUR LATER, I was washed and dressed in a fresh pair of black leggings, a worn T-shirt, and black hoodie. Now that the dragon had been freed and sent back to Alaska, New York was back to the crisp October fall weather I loved. Outside the walls of the Academy, the blaring of horns resumed as if the freak snow storm that'd brought the entire eastern seaboard to a stop never happened.

If Tuck wasn't lying in a bed fighting for his life, I might even say the sun shining down on me during a bright fall day was perfection. But he was fighting for his life, and though I wanted to stop and enjoy the courtyard like so many of the other students were, I just couldn't. I needed him to get better. Even now, I felt his turmoil in the pit of my stomach. It was a constant cramping pain no amount of Advil could cure.

I tossed my damp locks over my shoulder and marched from the library with the exact thing we needed. I pressed the book to my chest, holding it so tight I thought I might bruise my skin with the corner of it.

I was close to the middle of the courtyard in Evermore Academy when Beckett hopped in front of me. "What are you doing?"

He tossed his surfer blond hair back from his forehead, and those ocean-blue eyes of his sparked with life. We'd been through so much over the past few weeks, each of us fighting our own inner demons. On our last quest, Beckett nearly drowned, and before that, Grayson had been skinned by a siren. And now Tuck was lying there suffering whatever Alataris had done to him.

I was breathless and barely able to contain myself. "I think I've found something that'll help us."

A bright smile spread across his face. "That's the first good news we've had in a while."

"I know, right? Listen, can you get everyone together

and meet me in the library as soon as possible?" I took a few steps back. "I really think we can do—"

I spun on my heels and slammed right into a pillar. No, not a pillar. Someone's chest. The book fell to the ground, and I scrambled back. "I-I'm so sorry."

When I bent down to pick it up, a large hand scooped it up before I could. When I stood straight, I looked up and up and up. The boy towered over me like Beckett and Tuck did. He was at least six-foot-three, with straight dark hair falling to just above his chin. The sunlight reflected off of it, making it shine in ways I'd only seen in hair commercials. When he smiled down at me, his vivid gold eyes swallowed me whole. They were like two coins reflecting in the sun. I'd grown used to Tucker's warm honey eyes. Now looking up in these gold eyes, I didn't know if I should take a step back or start fanning myself.

He turned the book over and opened it to the page I had marked. "A black poppy prickle orchid." His dark eyebrows rose high on his forehead. "That's, um, some dark stuff you've got there. What do you think, Becks?"

He extended the book out to Beckett, whose jaw dropped open. "Cross, what are you . . . what are you doing here?"

Cross kept holding the book out. "Just came to see what all the fuss was about." He glanced around the courtyard where other students stopped to stare at him, particularly the girls. He was sleek and slender, wearing leather pants, biker boots, and a black V-neck T-shirt. A black leather jacket was draped over one of his arms, while he held the book out with the other.

Beckett stepped forward and engulfed the guy in a bear-like hug, clapping him hard on the back. "I'm so happy to see you, man."

I moved back, giving the two of them a moment. When they finally broke apart, I cleared my throat. "Um, hi. I'm Zinnia." I extended my hand out to him.

His fingers engulfed mine as he shook my hand. "Cross Malback."

"Nice to meet you, Cross." When he dropped my grip, I motioned to the book. "Can I have my book back?"

"Oh, yeah." He handed it over, then ran his hand through the silky strands of his hair. A deep chuckle escaped his lips. "Nice to meet me? Let me guess, you're the new one to Evermore?"

I pressed the book back to my chest. "What makes you say that?" I didn't want to be offended, but did I have newbie written across my forehead or something?

"No one says it's nice to meet a Malback. Let alone me. Isn't that right, Beck?"

"I don't know about that. I'm happy to see you, bruh.

36

It's been a long time." Beck reached over and took the book from my hands and opened it to the page where I'd placed my bookmark. "Zinnia, this is . . . something else."

When he glanced up at Cross, the two exchanged a look but said nothing. I reached over and pulled the book out of his hand. "What?"

Cross cleared his throat. "A black poppy prickle orchid is usually used on the darker side of magic. More specifically by warlocks." He narrowed his eyes at Beckett. "Isn't that right?"

Beckett nodded. "I believe so."

"I don't care if it is darker. If this is the only way to save Tuck, then we are doing it." I felt like a toddler about to have a tantrum just to get my way. "And what is the difference between a witch and warlock anyways? Aren't they the same?"

Beckett shifted from one foot to the other, kicking something on the ground. "No, not really. Witches deal in magic, the light kind. But warlocks, well, they are all dark magic."

"Like Alataris?" *Dear old Dad.* Yet another secret I had to keep. First my soul mate mark, then my family. If anyone looked close enough, they'd see it plain as day. *What would they all think? Would they trust me? Would Tuck?* A ball of dread sank in the pit of my stomach. *What if they turn their backs on me? What if he does?*

Again, they gave each other another look. Was I missing something? Cross tossed his jacket over his shoulder. "Exactly."

"I don't care. This is the answer we've been looking for. If we grind up the right pieces of the flower and put it into this potion I found and use it on Tuck, it'll remove any essence of evil in him." Hope was a dangerous emotion to have. It could make me think anything was possible. But in the end if it didn't work, the disappointment would be that much worse.

"Yeah, but this potion could also kill him. That flower is as poisonous as it could be helpful." Cross motioned to the book. "And the amount of dark magic needed to make it work would take someone very powerful. Isn't that right, Beck?"

I looked from one to the other and back again. "How do you know all this?"

"Well, well, well, if it isn't the prodigal badass son. What brings you out of private tutoring and into Evermore Academy?" Patty Pinch Face sauntered up to the three of us with her two brainless followers behind her: Carrie, who had a forehead a helicopter could land on and short frizzy black hair, and Laura, the other follower, whose words were limited to "that's right" and "yeah, Patty," had stringy dull blond hair. Each of them followed Patty around like a dog begging for treats at the table. If it wasn't so annoying, it'd be sad.

A half mocking smile pulled at Cross's lips. "Patricia Bowergaurd." He rolled his eyes. "A pleasure, as always."

Patty pursed her lips and moved in closer to him. "Cross, it's good to see you. Maybe stop by my room later." She placed her hand on his chest. "We'll hang out like we used to."

With two fingers, Cross plucked Patty's hand away from his chest. "Let's leave history where it belongs . . . in the past."

Patty's lips curled into a sneer as she looked at me. "Don't tell me you're into this one." She motioned to me. "A queen not even worthy of the name."

I stepped forward, about to say something, but Cross moved between us. "Queens are born, Patty, not bred. Even if they were, I doubt you'd make the cut." He made a show of looking her up and down. "After all, class can't be taught . . . clearly."

"Ouch." I giggled. "Better run along before he really tells you the truth."

Patty spun away from us and marched to the other side of the courtyard with her lackeys in tow.

Cross sighed. "Sometimes the sins of our past should stay there."

"I couldn't agree more." Beckett patted Cross on the

shoulder, then turned toward me. "I'll gather everyone in the library. Meet you there in five minutes?"

"Sure. Actually let's meet in the infirmary. I want to check on Tuck."

Beckett gave me a small salute, then strode away, leaving us alone.

I glanced around at the other students watching us. "Apparently, there is a lot about Evermore I don't know."

"Yeah, and before anyone else tells you, I might as well get this out there." Cross met my eye. "My father is Dario Malback . . . Alataris' right-hand man."

I sucked in a deep breath and wanted to turn away from him. How could I trust anyone that close to Alataris? But then I remembered just because the blood ran in his veins didn't make him evil. If that were the case, then I'd be just like *my* father. I threw my shoulders back and looked up at him. I hadn't noticed it before, but Cross too was holding his breath.

"Good thing who our parents are doesn't define who we are, right?" I gave him half a smile, hoping to reassure him.

"You say that like you know what it's like to be from the wrong side of everything."

I shrugged. "Maybe I do." Before he could ask any more questions, I took a step back. "I gotta go. But maybe we'll catch up later."

"Yeah, catch you later." When he turned from me, I could've sworn I saw something dark behind those gold eyes.

Perhaps the apple didn't fall so far from the tree in his family after all.

CHAPTER 4

ZINNIA

"What is with oversized dog?" Brax crossed his arms over his chest while staring down at Kumi with his feline green eyes. Last night he'd been in his pajamas. Now he was back into his army fatigues, with a black long-sleeved thermal shirt that fitted to his massive body and black cargo pants with pockets filled with only the Creator knew what. Tiny holes marred the torso of his shirt, giving everyone a glimpse of his skin.

Tell him he stinks. A mixture of kitty litter and puppy piss. Kumi's words drifted through my mind as though they were my own.

I will not. I turned toward Brax. "She's keeping watch over Tuck. Anyone else decides to lay a single hand on him and she won't hesitate—"

To rip your balls off.

I wanted to snicker at her sassy attitude, but I kept it to myself. I didn't need anyone else knowing I could hear her thoughts. It was a bit much on the weird scale, even for me.

Stop it.

Kumi blew out a sigh at my feet and laid her head across her paws. Nova sat on the cot next to Tuck. She held her hands over his torso with her eyes closed. Purple sparks flew from her fingertips, bounced off his chest, and landed back in her palms. I wasn't sure what she was doing, but I was captivated. The rest of the crew sat in the other cots surrounding him. We were in a loose circle with Tuck at the center.

Niche held the book I'd found in her hand and was thumbing through the pages quickly. "This really is interesting, Zin."

"I thought so. We have the chance to stop this hex and save him." I gazed down at Tuck, watching as he thrashed on the cot. "Every moment we hesitate he gets worse."

Nova dropped her hands. "I agree. He's there, but he's fighting. I can feel his soul . . . He's struggling." She tucked a lock of her white-blond hair behind her ear, then tugged her elbow-length gloves back into place.

I knew it in my bones he was struggling, but to hear

it out loud sent a chill down my spine and I was growing desperate to save him. "We have to go now."

Brax leaned over and extended his hand toward Kumi. "So soft."

Kumi's lips pulled back from her teeth, and a low growl rumbled deep in her chest. *Hands off, bub. I'm not a house pet.*

You could be a little nicer. These are my friends. I wanted to walk over and place Brax's hand on her soft fur. Yet I stayed where I stood, in the middle of them all, waiting for Niche or someone to tell me they would help me do this, help me find the way to save my Tucker. No matter the cost. I held my hand out to stop him. "I wouldn't if I were you."

Brax hesitated only a fraction of a second before he reached out and put his hand on her head. "Big puppy, da?" He was almost transfixed by her softness.

Did he just call me—a Kumiho, a devourer of men—a puppy? Her ears pressed flat against her head, and she snarled at him even louder.

Careful or they'll lock you in that room again. Besides, he's not going to hurt you.

Kumi stopped growling at him and sat still as a statue while the big Russian ran his fingers through the midnight fur on the top of her head over and over again. A soft smile played on his lips.

"See? Big dogs are not afraid of me."

Dog? Really?

When I looked down at her, she rolled her eyes but kept on sitting still.

Nova moved closer to me. "You didn't like riding Cerberus, but you have a Kumiho as your familiar. Tell me how that makes sense?"

"My what? And Cerberus was a three-headed giant wolf dog with teeth the size of my body. He was kind of scary. Kumi is pretty." I didn't want to say it out loud, but there was something deep in me that instantly trusted her. Like we'd always been together and always would be.

"Your familiar. It's rare for witches to have them, but it appears you do. This is an animal who helps us, guides us, protects us, and keeps us company through our lives. Usually it's a cat or a dog, not a mythological creature. But hey, you've never done anything the traditional way."

"True enough."

Niche turned the book around for all of us to see. "Look at this." She held up a picture of the flower I'd found. The orchid was black as night with vivid purple veins running through the petals. Each petal curled back from the yellow poppy seeds at the center of it and was tipped with a sharp point like a thorn at the end of it.

"To get the ingredients to help Tuck, we will need the whole flower. It'll have to be dissected just so, otherwise the poison within the veins and the seeds will seep into his body and kill him. Even more difficult, it's located in the Amazon, where very few supernaturals will dare go. We might live four times longer than humans and are twice as strong, but there are real dangers there that could hurt or kill any of you."

Beckett shrugged. "How is that different than any other day? We're always in danger, also threatened by death. Hell, three of us have already been knocking on death's door. I say we go. You say this plant can kill him. Well, I hate to say this, but we all know he's already dying."

I didn't want to hear it. I didn't want to hear he was dying or that he would die. In my mind, I couldn't think that way. Tuck had to live. If he didn't—no, there was no *if*. He would live, because I needed him, and he needed me. We were too young, had just barely started finding out what we could be. *I can't be without you.*

"Niche, how can we get there? To get the flower, I mean." I began pacing back and forth, then turned toward Beckett. "Can you portal us there?"

He shook his head. "I can only portal to places I've been or if someone shows me where I need to go. Like when Nova showed me a clear picture of Alaska. It's not like I can look in a book or Google it either. That's not how it works." He glanced around at the rest of us. "Has anyone been to the Amazon?"

We all shook our heads.

"There has to be some way to get us there."

Niche leapt to her feet. "I think I have an idea. Meet me in the courtyard in half an hour."

CHAPTER 5

ZINNIA

"You want us to do what now?" I looked down at the black combat boots covering my feet, then back up at where Niche stood. Kumi was lying by my side with her legs stretched out. Her breaths were slow and even. Her tails swished in all different directions. Even as calm as she appeared, I knew she was on alert, could feel it in the back of my mind.

"If you want to get to the Amazon within record time, then this is our only option." Niche motioned to the mysterious man standing beside her. If I passed him on the street, I wouldn't have even looked twice. He was average height, about five-foot-ten, slender, with light brown hair parted down the middle of his head. The straight locks fell onto the sides of his face like a '90s boyband wannabe. When Niche motioned to him, he didn't even look up from his cell phone. His thumbs flew across the screen in a blur of activity.

Grayson strolled up next to me. "I thought cell phones didn't work within the walls of the school."

The man paused for only a moment when he looked up at Gray. "Child's play."

"Who's this?" I crossed my arms over my chest. "Why can't Professor Brown send us like she did when she sent Tuck and me to Alataris' island?"

"Because, she'd been held prisoner there before. All she needed was his exact location. Professor Brown has never been to the part of Peru you all need to go," Niche snapped back at me. She glanced down at the clipboard in her hand and bit down on her bottom lip.

I don't like this. Kumi's words breathed through my mind.

Me neither. But what choice do I have?

She lifted one of her furry shoulders and let it drop. *Let him die?*

Kumi! He's my soul mate. If he dies . . .

Fine, fine. Don't let him die. If you go all sour, then I'll have to live with it for life, and I'd rather not. She gave one of those puppy groans as she sat up a little straighter.

For life? What are you talking about?

When I gazed down at her, she met my eye, and her

violet eyes swirled. *Because I'm your familiar . . . till death do us part.*

Okay, then as my familiar I need you to help me out and go keep an eye on Tuck. Make sure no one gets to him.

With a huff, Kumi rose from her comfy position on the ground and trotted off in the direction of the infirmary. Once she was out of view, I turned back toward Niche. "Still doesn't answer the question. Who is this?"

The man's head snapped up once more. This time when he turned those eyes on me, I took a small step back. They weren't the eyes of a normal human or any other supernatural I'd seen. Within those chutney colored eyes was a swirling mass of silvery flecks that held untold secrets from the ages. "Who am I? Who the hell are you?"

Grayson cleared his throat and leaned in closer to me. "Hermes, love. That's Hermes. To the human world, he'd be the Greek god of travelers and athletes."

"You're forgetting thieves and messenger to the other gods among other things. Though Matteaus and the other Fallen will tell you we aren't gods." He snickered. "Though we were once worshiped like we were."

I groaned. The last thing I needed to do was insult one of the most powerful supernaturals to walk the Earth. "I meant no offense."

As I looked him up and down, I should've known he

was powerful. Yes, he was slender, but there were muscles under that plaid button-down shirt. Though he wore only beige shorts, I should've noticed the thick black-winged tattoos that rose up from his ankles, covered his calves, and stopped at the back of his knees. He wasn't as dynamic as Poseidon or Hades, but there was a powerful undercurrent in the way he held himself.

He put his phone is his pocket and faced me fully. "Oh, I'm not offended. Just remember the next time you hit send when you're texting your little friends it's because of me they get the message. You think these"— he held his fingers up and made air quotes—"'wireless companies' would have any service without me?"

I hesitated. "Um, no?"

"No, that's right. And don't even get me started on the whole Prime thing, packages delivered the next day. Who ever heard of such a thing? Me, that's who. So, you are welcome." He pulled his cell back out of his pocket and started typing once more.

"Thank you?" I didn't know what I was supposed to say to him. Should I thank him for my cell service and overnight packages?

He didn't look up. "You're welcome. Now, Niche, why am I here?"

Niche cleared her throat and pushed the thick

glasses perched on her nose higher. "We need to get to Peru. The boiling river in the Amazon, to be exact."

Beckett moved to my other side and leaned in close to me. "What's he gonna do . . . mail us?"

I jabbed my elbow into his ribs. "Shh, let's not piss off the Greek until we know what's happening."

"Yes, let's not." Hermes sucked in a deep breath, then rubbed his hands together. "This is what we're going to do . . . Actually, everyone right this way."

Hermes bent down and placed his palm on the ground, then slowly lifted it. A door began to form from the ground up. A large metal one with rounded corners and a porthole like a window stood before us. A long metal lever sat in the middle of it. Hermes wrapped his hand around the lever and pulled it to the side. Air hissed from beyond the door as he pulled it open. I peeked through the open doorway. "Is that a portal?"

"Does it look like a portal?" Hermes motioned to it. "It's a door. Honestly, what are you teaching these kids?" He rolled his eyes at Niche.

Matteaus moved out from under the overhang around the courtyard. His large black wings were folded in close to his body, peeking out over the top of his shoulders. The sun reflected off the slick black feathers, giving them an oily effect. Though it was October now and the temperature was crisp, he still wore his tight black tank top with black army pants and combat boots. "Hermes!"

Hermes' eyes flashed wide for a split second before he turned toward Matteaus. "Yes, boss?"

"Don't *yes, boss* me. You know what I'm about to say." Matteaus marched across the courtyard and stood before Hermes, looking every bit the warrior he was, with leather straps running across his body, each one holding different sized blades.

Hermes sucked in a deep breath, then blew it out. "Make sure they get there alive?"

Matteaus stepped in closer to him. If Hermes had been taller, they would've been nose to nose. Instead, Matteaus was about five inches taller, with a good seventy-five pounds on Hermes. Matteaus spoke through thinned lips. "Make . . . sure . . . they . . . get . . . there . . . alive!"

Alive? What did that mean? A nervous ball turned in my stomach. "Has anyone not gotten where they needed to alive?"

Hermes looked at me over his shoulder and waved his hand back and forth. "Eh, kind of."

Matteaus lifted his hand and pointed a finger in his face. "No *kind ofs*. If anything happens to them on your watch, then you'll be answering to me and I will end your immortal life." He snapped his fingers. "Like that.

We clear?"

"Crystal." Hermes saluted him, then turned to the rest of us and waved us toward the door. "All aboard."

Niche pulled an oversized backpack from off her shoulder. Her body tilted forward with the lumbering weight as she handed it to Brax. "This has supplies in it for you all, in case anyone is injured or hungry or anything."

Brax wrapped his hand around the strap of the backpack and tossed it over his shoulder as though it weighed nothing. "I got it."

I moved toward the door and ducked my head as I passed through. The rest of the crew lined up behind me, ready to enter. Hermes slapped his hand across the entrance. "Wait a second. This isn't a school bus, kids. There's only enough room for five of you."

I spun on my heels and shoved his arm out of the way. "Five? That's all?"

"Unless you want this puddle jumper to go down, then by all means everyone pile on in." He motioned for the rest of the crew to move through the doorway.

When I glanced around, I sucked in a shocked breath. *How is this possible?* I stood in the entryway of a luxury jet. Plush tan leather seats were set up like captain's chairs, mahogany tables glinted in the sunlight, and the carpet under my feet cushioned my every step. I ducked my head down and looked out the window, expecting to see the school. Instead, I saw an open field filled with golden swaying grass. "We're not in Kansas anymore . . ."

After all the time I'd spent in Evermore Academy, I should've been used to the magic of portals and travel. But to me I still didn't understand it all. Hermes could use magic to get us into a plane but not directly to the Amazon?

Outside, Hermes' voice boomed. "Choose your champions. We haven't got all day."

I turned on my heels and marched out of the plane. "We don't have much time. Brax, Tabi, Nova, Beckett, let's go." I motioned for them to go through the door.

Grayson sped to my side. "You sure you don't need me?"

I looked him dead in the eye. "Nope, we're good. See you when we get back."

Brax grabbed ahold of Grayson's shirt and yanked him in close. He murmured so low in his ear I couldn't make out the words.

Grayson leaned back on his heels and looked up at him. "You can't be serious."

Brax backed away from him and pointed at his chest. "Make sure it happens."

"Fine." Gray rolled his eyes and walked away.

One by one, the others filed onto the plane. I stepped in front of Brax and pressed my hand to his chest. "What was that about?"

"Don't worry about it." He pushed past me, then dropped himself down into one of the plush leather seats.

Tabi, our Queen of Elements, sat down in the chair across from Brax. "Are you okay?"

"Da. I'm fine." He shifted in his chair, looking out the window with a scowl on his face.

Tabi brushed her wild ebony curls away from her face. They made her hazel eyes look even brighter against her mocha skin. Though we were traveling to the Amazon, she wore skin-tight olive cargo pants, thick black work boots, and a white tank top covered by a thin black mesh shirt. "You don't look fine."

Brax's brows furrowed, and he slouched down in his chair. When he crossed his arms over his chest, his shirt pulled tight on his biceps. He pressed his lips together and didn't answer. I could relate to his mood. I didn't want to go either. Most of all, I didn't want to leave Tucker behind. This would be the first mission without him, and it was the most important mission of all . . . to save my soul mate.

Hermes yanked the door shut and slid the handle to the side. The hiss of air that came afterward told me we were sealed inside. Hermes clapped his hands together as he walked down the center aisle of the plane. "Hold on to your asses."

Was that a smirk? Before I could get a closer look, he shoved through the cockpit door and slammed it behind him. There was only a moment before his voice came over the loudspeaker. "Ladies and gentlemen, thank you for choosing Greek Airlines. This is your captain speaking, the undeniably adventurous Hermes. Lavatories will be in the back of the plane. Stick to number ones, folks."

"Ugh, gross." Tabi wrinkled her nose while she shook her head.

Hermes cleared his throat. "Our trip will be about four hours."

"Four hours? I thought this was going to be at least a ten-hour flight." I leaned over the table and caught Beckett's eye. "How is that possible?"

Beckett gazed out the window. "They're some of the most powerful supernaturals in the world." He shrugged. "Anything is possible."

The engines whirred to life. A low hum filled the plane, and that momentary nervousness I always felt before flying overcame me. My mother and I traveled all over the country for what I thought was work. Only a few weeks ago I found out she was hiding me from a madman, my father. Now I'd faced off against Alataris more times than I would like, but I always had Tuck by my side. This time, we would have to move forward without our leader. My heart sank to think about him lying in that bed fighting for every breath he took. I closed my hand into a tight fist and dug my nails into my palm. He wouldn't want me to be sad or scared now. Not when he needed me the most.

The outside world sped by as we gathered speed. I sank deeper into my seat as we lifted off the ground.

Hermes came over the loudspeaker once more. "I don't really care if your seats are in their upright and locked positions. If the seat belt sign is on, do what you want. If you crack your skulls on the ceiling, not my problem."

I fumbled for my seat belt and pulled it tight across my lap. The plane climbed higher, and I dug my fingers into the arms of the chair as my ears plugged up to an uncomfortable degree.

Nova dropped into the seat next to mine. "You okay?"

Am I okay? Not in the slightest. When it banked to the side, my stomach dropped to my toes.

This is going to be a long flight.

CHAPTER 6

I pressed both my hands to my temples, staring down at the book in front of me. I wanted to remember every inch of that flower. I needed to be able to identify it, grab it, and get back to Tuck. But the more I stared at it, the worse I felt. Dizziness overcame me each time the plane changed directions. My stomach wanted to empty its contents, and my head was pounding. "Ugh, no wonder my mom always gave me pills before we left for a trip. Motion sickness is no joke."

Nova reached across the table and pulled the book out from in front of me. "It's worse if you keep focusing on a book. Sit back and try to relax. We're almost there."

She tossed the book to Brax. "Put that in the pack."

Without a word, he slid the book into the backpack, zipped it up tight, and shoved his arms back through the loopholes. When he leaned back in his seat, the lower half of his body stuck out a little from the bag behind him.

I motioned to the book. "Brax, why don't you put it on your lap?"

"Must keep it at all times. Niche said." He shrugged and leaned his head back against the chair and closed his eyes.

Not much for conversation. I turned away from him and glanced out the window. I could see we were getting closer. The landscape had changed, and lush green mountains were broken up by wide rivers. The water was a brownish-red color and flowed freely in multiple directions. In the distance, steam rose up from the ground as though a volcano were nearby. "So this boiling river, anyone know why it's boiling? I was under the impression there weren't any volcanos around here."

"Oh, there aren't." Nova looked down at her phone. "Some locals believe there's a river spirit there causing the water to boil; others believe there's a two-headed serpent, one that spouts both cold water and scalding hot. If you fall into the river, the spirit instantly collects your soul."

"How do you know all that?" My eyes widened.

She held her phone up. "Google."

I rolled my eyes. "I should've known. Note to self, avoid the river serpent."

"Well, that and my caste taught me about it. I just wanted to see what the human legends were." She shrugged and tucked it back into her pocket.

"What did the death caste say about it?" I swallowed around the nervous ball in my throat, wanting a distraction from my constant worrying over Tuck.

She slid deeper into the chair and sighed. "In truth, it's both. There is a river serpent that lies at the mouth of the river spouting both cold and boiling water. It's invisible to the human eye because it's like a chameleon. Its skin blends in with its surroundings. They work together."

Beckett groaned. "I hate river serpents, with all their teeth, and eyes, and how they like to swallow you whole."

"You know this particular serpent?" There was so much about this world I had to learn about. I was always behind.

He met my eye. "No, but one encounter with one of them was enough. If it weren't for Tuck . . ." A wistful smile played on his lips. "I would've died in the Trials to become a knight."

Tuck. Even hearing his name sent me back into a panic. "Really? I had no idea."

"Oh yeah. I knew after that we'd be friends. He didn't let any of us get hurt. He was amazing."

"I bet." Tears pricked at the back of my eyes, and I fought not to let them drop down my cheeks.

Nova leaned forward and patted my hand. "You okay?"

"Yeah, it'll be fine. We'll find the flower and we will save him." I pressed my lips together, determined to do anything to save him . . . *anything.*

"I know he was the first one of us you met. You guys have always had something special. We all know it. We'll all do everything we can. He's our leader, Zin. We'll be there for him too."

"I know." I brushed my hair out of my face. "Tell me more about the boiling river." I needed a distraction before my emotions got the better of me.

Nova smiled. "According to what my elders taught me, the spirit feeds the serpent in exchange for a peaceful afterlife."

"What do you mean he feeds it?" I didn't like the sound of that at all.

"It knocks animals and people into the water. It's so hot that it instantly kills them." She tucked a long strand of her white-blond hair behind her ear. "Then he brings them to the serpent so it can stay within its den. You know they say that particular serpent is a homebody. If it has to leave its nesting area . . . well, let's just say vicious doesn't even begin to describe it."

Note to self: don't fall in or wake the evil sea snake.

"That would explain why you could only get the flower here." I turned around to see Hermes standing in the aisle. This time, he wore a brown one-piece jumper that cut off at his knees and was held together by a thick silver zipper that ran from below his stomach all the way up to his neck. He had a pair of goggles perched on top of his head. My mouth dropped open. Why was he standing here? He cleared his throat and continued. "Like I was saying, that flower can probably only grow on that particular river because it drinks boiling water and needs the steaming heat to survive."

"If you're standing here, who's flying the plane?" I leapt to my feet just as the plane started to drift downward. My body was thrown sideways. I stumbled and fell into one of the mahogany tables. I threw my arms out to catch myself, but it was too late. I hit my side on the corner of the table, then fell to the floor.

My heart hammered in my chest as I rolled and sat up just in time to watch Hermes march toward the door in the cabin. He gave me a salute. "Happy landing."

Brax jumped up and reached for him. He wrapped his hand in the back of Hermes' collar. "Matteaus said for us to get there alive."

Hermes twisted free of his grip and smiled. "I have no doubt you will." He shoved Brax back, then wrapped his hand around the handle and yanked it, opening the door.

Wind filled the cabin, sending my already wild hair to fly into my face. Those small black tattoos on his calves peeled away from his skin and started to flutter like wings on a humming bird. There was no way I was going to let him leave us like this. I gathered a ball of my silvery magic in my hands and threw it at his leg. Just before he leapt out the door, it smacked into his leg, exploding one of those little wings in a puff of black feathers. I shoved to my feet and raced to the window to watch him plummet toward the ground as he spun in wild directions.

Tabi grabbed my arm and yanked me around to meet her panicked face. "What should we do?"

I glanced at all my friends as they all looked at me. *This is what Tuck feels like every day. God, the pressure.* I sucked in a deep breath, reaching for a calm I didn't feel. "Does anyone know how to fly a plane?"

They all stared at me blankly. *Shit.*

"Okay." I pressed my hand to my head. The plane dropped out from under us. My body flew up and smacked into the ceiling before hitting the ground again. I struggled up to my hands and knees and pointed toward the door. "That's it! Beckett, make a platform."

"Where? It's not big enough in here, and we're going down." He spun in a circle, and his eyes bulged out of his head.

"Outside the door. We all jump, now." I hurried to my feet and grabbed Nova's hand. "Let's go." I dragged her down the aisle behind me.

The lights in the plane flashed, and the metal groaned and shook. "Becks, now."

He raced forward and made a blue ball of magic in his hands. He expanded it until it was a large flat disk. "He nodded at me, you ready?"

"Ready."

He shoved it out the open door, and I raced forward with Nova behind me. We leapt out of the plane onto the thin blue disk. I smacked into it hard and dropped Nova's hand. The surface was smooth like glass and hard as marble. I slid across it and off the edge. At the last second, I grabbed on with the tips of my fingers. My legs dangled thousands of feet in the air, and the wind whipped around me, knocking my body in all different directions. "Pull me up!"

Just then, the plane arched and dove straight toward the ground. Two meaty hands wrapped around my wrist and yanked me back onto the platform. Brax held me up in front of him. "Don't do that again, da?"

Not like I wanted to hang thousands of feet off the side of a magical disk only seconds away from dropping to my death. I breathlessly nodded. "I won't."

He pressed his lips into a thin line, then placed me on my feet next to Nova. There we were huddled together on a blue platform in the middle of the sky with gusting winds ready to knock us off. Though the sun was blinding above us, the harsh winds made it colder.

Beckett stood off to the side, holding his hands out with his eyes closed tight. "What now?"

When I opened my mouth to answer, I was cut off by the plane crashing into the side of a smaller mountain. It exploded into a ball of fire. Smoke billowed up from it in a cloud of what would've been our deaths. "Hermes," I growled like a curse.

"Yeah, but you hit him before he bailed on us." Nova wrapped her arm around my shoulder and squeezed.

"Wasn't enough." Not nearly enough. His name was on my shit list, and one day I'd make him pay.

"Guys, don't know how much longer I can hold five of us suspended in midair. We need a plan." Sweat trickled down the sides of Beckett's face, and his body quaked with the effort he was using to keep us afloat.

Tabi moved to his side and wrapped her fingers in

his hand. "Just ease up a bit and I can help you drift us down."

Tendrils of her magic seeped from her fingers in yellowy bands that flowed over the top of the platform and dropped off the edge. The wind stopped whipping from side to side and whirled straight up. Tabi closed her eyes and held her hands out. "Okay, Beck. Let the wind steer us."

The second he did, I felt it. We went from standing on solid ground to shaking. I spread my footing and held my hands out to keep my balance. "You guys got this."

The platform vibrated and sloped slightly as we moved toward the ground. Fire caught on the trees surrounding the plane, and smoke covered the ground for miles. It mixed in with the steam from the forest. My heart sank. How would we know where to go now? We moved at a snail's pace, all the while I looked around trying to figure out where exactly we were.

Then something large smacked into the side of us, knocking the platform out from Tabi's wind tunnel. We tilted like a seesaw, back and forth. "What was that?"

Hermes threw one arm over the edge of the platform. "You messed with my wings. Bad idea, little girl."

"You tried to kill us." I held my hands out for balance. The platform continued to waver as he repeatedly tried to throw his leg over the side and pull himself up.

"This has to stop now," Beckett growled.

"I agree." I took unsteady steps to get to Hermes.

He smiled up at me. "I didn't try to kill you. You're here, aren't you?" He reached his hand out to me. "Now help me up. Matteaus won't like it if I tell him you hit me with magic and tried to kill me."

"Tried to kill you?" I narrowed my eyes at him and squatted down. "You left five teenagers in a plane to crash and die."

"I knew you'd live." He shook his hand at me. "Grab it."

"Oh, I'm not worried about you, Hermes. I know you'll live." I kicked my leg out and connected with his chin, sending him flying back off the edge of the platform.

"Zinnia, no!" Nova raced up beside me. "You didn't."

"Everyone stop moving now!" Beckett yelled at the top of his lungs. His hands shook, and his eyes flashed wide-open. "Oh, crap."

The magical platform disappeared beneath our feet. My stomach rose up into my chest, and we all plummeted.

CHAPTER 7

NOVA

"**I**s everyone okay?" I could barely catch my breath as the branch I was draped over dug into my stomach. My hair fell in a curtain over my face, blinding me to my surroundings. The smell of damp earth, leaves, and woods filled my senses. The sound of a waterfall filled the air with a peaceful hum. Beads of sweat gathered on my skin. My gloves stuck to me in ways no clothing should stick, yet I couldn't take them off.

"Ughhhh, everything hurts."

I pressed up on the branch and shoved my hair from my face. "Zinnia?"

"Yeah, it's me." Her voice sounded strained, like she too was tangled up.

"Where are you?" I twisted my head around, looking in every direction on the ground.

The branches over my head rustled. "I'm above you."

"Damn it." I swung one of my legs over the limb and slowly twisted until I was straddling it. The bark scratched into the tops of my arms. "That's better."

"Speak for yourself."

I titled my head back and back and back. There was Zinnia hanging upside down with her foot caught in a vine. Her arms dangled down beside her midnight hair.

"Oh my God, hold on, Zin." I glanced around and tried to scramble to my feet. I swung my legs back and pushed up while holding myself with my arms. Slowly, I came to a stand like a tightrope walker with my arms out.

"Are you crazy? You can't walk across a tree branch." She jostled around. A scream broke past her lips as she dropped ten feet before she yanked to a stop.

"Stop moving!" I held my hand up.

"Okay, okay," she whispered. She held her arms stiffly. "I'm not moving."

"Zinnia!" Beckett came to a skidding halt below the tree, followed by Brax and Tabi. They were covered in dirt and a little scratched up, but all were alive and well.

A smile spread across my face. "Becks! Oh, thank the Creator."

Zinnia swung her head around. Her midnight locks swirled in a tangled mess. "Becks, is that you?"

"Stop moving, Zin. Just stop!" He glanced around them and shoved Brax right underneath her. "Stay here."

"Screw this. I'm coming down. Brax, get ready." Zinnia summoned her blade to her hand. The brilliant white light shined in her palm for only a moment, then the rounded blade formed in her hand. She wrapped her fingers around the straight end that connected the whole thing.

My hands shook as I tiptoed across the thick branch. "No, don't."

She swung her body up and swiped at the vine around her ankle. She severed only half of the thick green vine. "Damn." She swung up again. This time, the blade went clear through and she dropped thirty feet down toward Brax's waiting arms.

He ran forward with his arms extended. I held my breath as she fell into him. A painful groan escaped his lips as he fell backward with her in his grasp. They hit the ground in a twist of limbs.

I squatted down on the branch and waited for them both to get up. Zinnia was the first to pop to her feet and brush off her hands. I cupped my hands around my mouth. "Are you insane? You could've died."

She shook her head. "We're wasting time."

"Says the girl who kicked a Greek supernatural in the face. I don't think you're in the right mindset at the moment." It was true. Ever since Tuck was hexed, Zinnia had been getting closer and closer to crazy town. All my life I'd been a queen, the strongest one within the death caste, and yet I had no real connections to anyone. But ever since our last mission when Zinnia saved me from the pitfalls of my own powers, we were growing closer. I'd be damned if I lost the nearest thing I had to a best friend.

A shimmering pool of blue magic appeared next to me. Beckett strolled through it right onto the branch next to me. I'd always been taken with his good looks. Not that I liked him, but he was gorgeous in a hot surfer with a darker edge kind of way. His ocean-blue eyes nearly matched his portal, and his dirty-blond hair was a wavy mess that fell around his tan skin. "Yeah, and if she only waited a second longer I could've just portalled her down instead of taking unnecessary chances."

I nodded. "That's right."

"Gee, Mom and Dad, are you going to ground me now?" Zinnia stomped her foot. "Now get down here. We have to get moving!"

Beckett extended his hand out toward me. "Shall we go?"

I tugged my gloves higher up my arms, ensuring they were in place before I touched him. I shivered to think what would happen if I even brushed his skin against mine. "Yes, let's."

I followed him through his portal. One moment I was wobbling on a branch, the next I was drifting through his pool of magic. It was one of the more violent portals I'd been through, where I felt like I was being yanked and pulled in harsh directions and spinning in rapid circles before I stepped out on the other side. I teetered on my feet for only a moment, then I found my footing on the leaf-covered ground.

Zinnia paced back and forth in front of me. She ran her hands through her wild windblown hair, muttering to herself. "How are we going to find the flower now? No plane, no plan, no direction to go in. Damn it, Zin. Think." She pressed her hands to her temples, looking like she was trying to hold her emotions in.

Through this whole thing, I felt there was something more going on between her and Tuck. We all wanted to save him, but Zinnia was on the razor's edge of going insane while trying. "Calm down. It'll be okay."

She spun on her heels and faced off against me. "How exactly will it be okay?" Her sapphire eyes were wide with terror. "He is waiting for us. We've already wasted hours. Hours of time he's on the verge of losing."

I reached out and placed my hand on her shoulder. "He is strong. I felt it. Now we have to be too."

Unshed tears swam in her eyes. "How are we going to find that flower now? We don't even know where the boiling river is, or where the flower is along it."

Then it hit me. For years I'd seen Niche use one of the oldest witching techniques known and for years I'd never tried it. I reached out my hand toward Brax. "I need your pack now."

Without hesitation, he handed it over to me. The moment he let go, I tipped forward and the pack dragged my arm down to the ground. I narrowed my eyes at him. "Really?"

"You asked for it." Brax, our gentle giant, was hulking and massive. I should've known better, but I was too focused on what we needed. I squatted down and began unzipping the pack. All around me, leaves rustled. Whether it was wild animals or just the wind, I didn't know. I opened my senses, wanting to know exactly what we were up against. The sheer amount of souls surrounding us was overwhelming. I froze. "No one make any sudden movements."

Zinnia looked over her shoulder. "Why? What's happening?"

"We are surrounded by a lot of animals, some curious, some waiting to see who will be the first to die." To my left, a large snake slithered across the ground. Sensing a predator, it kept on moving. Up in the trees all around us, monkeys waited to steal something from us. They too held off, sensing a powerful animal.

"Brax, they're scared of you." I motioned to our audience. When he pursed his lips and crossed his arms over his chest, I shrugged. "What?"

"I'm tired of furry creatures being scared of me." He kicked at a stone on the ground.

"Well, this time it's going to keep us from being hunted by some big game, so if you could please just shift?" I dipped my hand into the pack, searching for what I needed.

"Maybe I don't want to shift. Maybe I want them to like me." Tiger stripes spread across his neck and up his arms. His teeth extended into lengthy fangs.

"Oh, for the love . . ." Zinnia jabbed a finger into his chest. "You change now. We're not here to make friends with all the poisonous creatures of the Amazon." Then she swung her finger around toward me. "And you find what we need so we can go."

I looked up at her. "Patience is a virtue."

"One I don't have right now." She grabbed the bag from my hands and dumped its contents onto the ground at her feet. "What are we looking for?"

I rolled my eyes. "You know, sometimes it's hard to like a bossy pants, and I'm looking for a pendulum."

"Good thing I'm not worried if I'm liked right now."

She dropped down to her knees and started rummaging through all the things Niche had packed for us.

Fur sprang from Brax's body and he dropped to the ground. He turned into a tiger the size of a small car. He growled at Zinnia and swiped a paw at her. She spared him only a second glance. "Good kitty."

Again, he growled. All my life I'd been able to feel the emotions of animals. Not that I could hear them, but I could feel what they felt. And when shifters were in their animal form, the same applied, so when he turned toward me practically projecting his emotions, I couldn't stop from snickering. "He said two words. One of them started with an F. I'll give you one guess what the other was . . ."

"Good thing I don't speak kitten." She looked him in the eye. "I need you to protect us, and you're better at that in this form for now."

Beckett loomed over her and placed his hand on her shoulder. "We'll get back to Tuck. You don't have to be so harsh."

She shrugged him off. "I'm not being harsh. I'm telling the truth. We don't have time to stand here and debate this."

She didn't even look up at him. She just kept her eyes on the pile in front of us. Her hand darted out and snatched at something on the ground. "Found it." She held it out toward me. "Okay, do it."

I pressed my hand to my chest. "Me?"

"Yes, lead the way, Nova." She tossed the onyx stone at me.

I held it up by the thin chain it was attached to. *Okay, please let this work. Take me to the black poppy orchid, please.* And then the pendulum began to swing.

CHAPTER 8

" **A**re we there yet?" My patience was growing thin, and we had yet to see one orchid. I felt like a little kid on a road trip wanting to get to our destination but feeling like it'd be an eternity until I got there. Ahead of me, Nova took calm, sure steps. In this scenario, was she the parent and I the child?

She'd led us from where we'd crashed all the way through the thick, dense jungle to the boiling river, where we now walked along the banks. The air was so dense it was like sitting in a steam room. Pieces of my hair hung down the sides of my face in soaking tatters. The rest of it was in a messy knot on the top of my head. Whether it was from steam or sweat, I didn't know.

Nova had her hair braided down the side of her body, and sweat soaked her shirt and pants, yet she didn't take off those damn gloves. She glanced at me over her shoulder. "You know as much as I do."

Her voice was unruffled and steady like her steps. I couldn't decide if I was grateful she had her wits about her or if I was pissed she didn't feel the urgency I did to save Tuck. Beside us, Brax prowled in his tiger form, growling and hissing on occasion. Nova told us the animals were still at bay for now. They cowered in fear of our massive protector.

I felt like we'd been walking for hours, more hours than Tuck could spare. Exhaustion ate at my every step. I was hot, thirsty as hell, and hungrier than a bear after winter. Any moment, I was going to lose my shit. I had to turn my attention else- where or I would explode. Through our last adven- ture, I'd been scared but calm and steady because I had Tuck by my side. Now Nova seemed to be the anchor I needed to cling to. "Why do you wear those gloves?"

Nova's back stiffened for a fraction of a second before she took her next step. "Style choice."

"In this heat?" Tabi chimed in from behind me. "I've been wondering this for years. Is it really a fashion thing?"

Nova shrugged and pushed a low-hanging branch from in front of her. "It's part of my personal style. I don't ask why you wear bright colors or why Zin likes her combat boots, do I?"

Her voice wavered for only a second, but in that second, I could tell she was hiding something. Call it gut instinct, but I knew there had to be more to it. But I didn't want to push it. We all had our secrets. I glanced down at the bracelet wrapped around my wrist, hiding the soul mate mark. *Indeed, we all have our own secrets.* "Well, I like them."

She smiled over her shoulder at me, then mouthed the words "thank you." As we climbed over another set of weaving roots, large light-colored boulders rose up in front of us and began to run along both sides of the river banks. Steam seeped from between the cracks, the sun beat down on us, and a swarm of gnats were floating around my head. "Tabi, can you give us some AC?"

"If I could do that, we'd be in an arctic blast right now. But you know, I'd get drained and I need to preserve my powers in case we need them. I'm exhausted as it is." Pebbles skidded down the side of the boulder behind me, and Tabi cursed under her breath.

"Wishful thinking, I guess." I chuckled. As we climbed over another boulder, a shrill scream broke the silence of the jungle. I stopped short. "What was that?"

I didn't wait for anyone to answer. I ran around

Nova and headed right for it. I didn't know why, but something deep inside me drove me forward. I pushed through thick bushes and stumbled over a high root and fell to one knee in the middle of a scorched clearing. The light-colored boulders had black burn smudges all over them, and the sound of a large waterfall was nearly deafening.

"Zinnia, wait!" Nova called out after me.

I didn't turn back. Standing across the clearing with his back to me was the one person I dreaded seeing the most. He loomed over the edge, peering down at the waterfall. At what, I didn't know. "Alataris," I growled and rose to my feet.

He spun around, and a slow smile spread across his lips. "Zinnia, darling." He motioned to the area around him. "Funny seeing you here. Looking for something?"

Nova stepped through the bushes behind me. "Guys, we're here." She had yet to raise her gaze to Alataris. The pendulum in her hand spun in rapid circles, then flew in his direction and imbedded itself in the ground at his feet.

When she finally looked up, she sucked in a shocked breath. "Alataris." She held her hands out, and purple sparks gathered on her fingertips. "What are you doing here?"

Tabi shoved to her side and opened her hands.

Yellow ribbons of magic dove into the ground. Vines streamed out from all around Alataris and leashed around his ankles and wrists. She threw her arms wide, and the vines snapped tight, forcing his limbs away from his body like a starfish. When his hand was yanked away from behind his back, I saw the flash of the flower held within his fingertips.

I reached out toward him. "Give it to me." I took a step forward.

"Oh, you want this?" His eyes flashed with excitement. Though his wrists were bound, he could still wave that flower back and forth. Its petals fluttered with each of his movements, and I wanted to rip it from him.

I gathered my magic in my palms. Streams of silver swirled around my body and down my arms. Wickedness like I'd never felt before called to me. My hair blew back from my face and I held my arms high, ready to blast his ass to kingdom come. I didn't care if he lived or died by my hand. Yes, he was my father . . . he'd also tried to kill me on more than one occasion. *Turnabout is fair play, Dad.* "Give it to me now."

"Release me first." He narrowed his eyes on Tabi.

She shook her head. "Our policy is we don't negotiate with terrorists."

"Perhaps if I did this." A flame lit down his arms and

stopped at his wrists. The flame flickered only a millimeter away from the stem of the flower.

"Nobody move!" I held my hands out to my sides just as Beckett leapt into the clearing with Brax right behind him.

"Zin, what's happening?" Three blue orbs curled and spun through his fingers.

"He's got the flower we need." I pointed to the orchid Alataris clutched in his hand. "And it's the only one left here. I can only guess what happened to the rest."

A dark chuckle rumbled deep in his chest. "How is Tuck? Was that his name? Poor guy must be suffering something awful." He threw his head back, laughing toward the sun-kissed sky.

I took a step forward. "This is all your fault!" I wanted to fire everything I had at him. I wanted to take him down then and there. But then what would happen to Tuck? Would the hex die with the man who did it to him, or would he suffer even more? It wasn't something I was willing to chance.

Beckett let one of his orbs float out toward Alataris. "I say we kill him while we can."

"I like this one. He's ruthless. What's the last name again? Do I know your family?" Alataris turned his head to the side, looking him up and down. "Your features seem so familiar."

"Shut up." Beckett gritted his teeth, and the orbs began circling faster around Alataris' head.

"Give us the flower and we'll let you go." I took another step toward him and held my hand out for it. Though we were yards away, if he made any move to hand me the flower, I would go for it.

"Will you? How interesting." His eyes widened, and he looked me up and down. "If I told you I'd give you your mother back in exchange for the flower, what would you say?"

The air left my lungs in a rush. This man dangled the two people who mattered the most to me over my head. I hesitated. My mother or Tuck. I ground my teeth together. "You're a monster."

Magical fire spread across his body, severing the vines Tabi had holding him. When the flames died out, he still held the flower in his hand, and he gracefully paced back and forth on the edge of the waterfall. "That wasn't the question I asked. Choose now. Your mother or the flower."

"It's a trick, Zin. Don't listen to him." Beckett moved beside me. I stood torn between a rock and a hard place. Left with no other choice, I sprinted forward and summoned my blades to my hands as I ran.

"I'll kill you!" I pumped my arms and ran harder. The moment I closed in on him, I swung for his neck. He leaned back, dodging the blade by less than an inch. His black sword appeared in his hand, and he swung out, blocking my next advance. With one hand, he wielded his sword. With the other, he held that flower like a red flag in my face.

Again, I leaned forward, aiming for a killing blow, but he swung up. Steel clashed against steel as he blocked my strike. Sparks flew in different directions. I spun around and swung at his leg. My blade glided across his thigh, ripping his black pants and shredding through his skin. He stumbled back and pressed his free hand to his thigh. Blood streamed through his fingers. "Good. Now stop fighting with emotion and start using some skill."

A scream ripped up from my throat, and I leapt into the air, bringing both blades onto his sword. With one hand I aimed for his neck, and with the other I swung for his midsection. Alataris tilted back on his heel and kicked me in the chest, sending me flying back. My back smacked into a boulder, and the air rushed from my lungs, yet I couldn't stop, wouldn't stop. I would kill him for the things he did to the ones I loved.

He held the flower out in front of him. "Stop."

I froze. My breaths heaved in and out, and the muscles in my arms shook with the effort I'd been using against him. Steam wafted up from the cracks in the rocks, and a mist of water covered my skin from the waterfall. Off to the side, Nova called to Beckett, "Hit him now."

Alataris swung around and held the flower up. "If you want your friend to live, I wouldn't."

"He's right. Just stay there, Beck." I moved to face off against him once more. "Alataris, give me the flower."

If possible, Alataris' grin broadened. He tossed the flower into the air and then launched a ball of fire at it, charring it to ash. In the next second, he ran for the edge of the waterfall and leapt off the side.

"No!" I raced forward with my hands cupped in front of me. I dropped to my knees, trying to catch the ashes of what remained of our only hope of saving Tuck. The tears I'd been holding back fell from my eyes in rapid succession. I ran my fingers over the ground, covering them in ash and dust, yet nothing of the flower remained. Heaving sobs racked my chest, and I felt the world spin. *How could we lose? How could this happen?* Not one time did I think I'd lose him. Now crawling on the ground, unable to stop the gut-wrenching sobs wracking my body, I knew I'd just signed his death certificate.

"Guys!" Nova screamed. "We gotta go now."

I shook my head. "I can't."

"Snake! Snake! Snake!" Nova's voice rose over the

sound of the splashing water. A thunderous roar echoed through the clearing.

"Zinnia, come on." Beckett squatted down beside me and rested his hand on my shoulder. "Let's get back to the school now! We'll figure something else out. There's nothing left here for us."

I wrapped my hands around my torso and rocked back and forth, mumbling to myself, "Nothing left. I failed. I've lost him."

Tabi darted to the edge of the waterfall and lifted her arms, a wall of water rose up. A snake the size of a skyscraper rose. Its dual head loomed over the top of the water wall. Each one was modeled after a copper head with red stripes flowing back from the sides of its lips. When it opened its mouths, spouts of water gushed from each side. I turned away from it, wanting to curl in a ball and ignore it. *I lost him. He's going to die.*

My world was going to end, and it was all because of one man. First, he'd taken my mother, and now he was about to kill my soul mate. There was nothing I could do about either. Beckett wrapped one arm around my back and swiped his other under my legs. He lifted me up as though I weighed nothing. "Come on, let's go home."

"I have no home." There was nothing left for me. Alataris had taken it all away. My mother was gone, and now Tuck would be taken from me. Without him, Evermore Academy couldn't be called home.

"Guys! Now, we go now," Nova urged.

I didn't care about the stupid snake. I'd lost my only chance to save Tuck. Screaming rattled in my ears.

"Shh, I got you." The blue portal seemed to rise from out of nowhere.

My head fell onto Beckett's shoulder, and I suddenly felt tired down to my bones. The screaming stopped. *Was it mine? I think so.* I was tired of fighting, tired of all-consuming worry, and tired of fighting a losing battle. When he stepped through the portal, I stopped resisting my lids and let them drift closed.

CHAPTER 9

"How long is she going to be out?" I paced back and forth in front of Zinnia's bed in the infirmary. She'd been lying in the cot next to Tuck's for hours now. Though her injuries were limited to a few scratches and bruises, there was no reason for her to be out this long.

"She just needs some rest. It's been a long day for her." The doctor patted my shoulder and moved down to the aisle to the next patient. I wound my fingers together and wrung my hands and started the pacing all over again.

"Anything change?"

I jumped at the deep rumbling voice behind me. When I spun on my heels, Beckett looked down at me. He crossed his arms over his chest.

I shook my head. "Not since we got back. Beck, she looked so broken by the waterfall." My voice wavered. "And the screaming. I can't get it out of my head."

When I turned back toward them, Tuck continued to thrash on his cot. Sweat streamed off of him onto the soaked cot. "Maybe it's for the best. I don't think she could take looking at him like this for much longer."

Beckett shifted from one foot to the other. "Niche said that if we can't figure out what the hex was exactly, then . . ."

He didn't have to finish that sentence. We all knew what it meant for Tuck. I glanced toward Zinnia. Even now in her sleep, she reached out toward him. If we lost him, then we'd lose her too. And losing my closest friend wasn't an option. "Ugh. I'm about to show up on that island, bang on his door, and knock Alataris out, kidnap him and force him to tell us what the hell he did to Tuck."

Zinnia sat straight up in her bed. "That's it!"

I jumped back. My heart leapt up into my throat. "What's it?"

Zinnia scrambled out of the cot and grabbed my arms. Her fingers dug into my skin, pinching me. "We have to kidnap Alataris."

CHAPTER 10

ZINNIA

I knew I was grasping at straws. I knew this new plan was crazy, but I had nothing else to hold on to. I couldn't just lie down next to Tuck and watch him die. Not now, not ever. The rest of the crew was gathered before me. Kumi rested on the floor at the foot of Tuck's bed. Though her eyes were closed, her tails swished back and forth, telling me she was as alert as I was. I'd taken a total of ten minutes to shower, get dressed, and get back to the infirmary where we all now sat.

The doctor pushed past Grayson and Brax, who were blocking the aisle. "You kids could meet someplace else, you know?"

I ignored him as I sat perched on the edge of my cot. The infirmary was quiet, and no one dared to interrupt us with Kumi lying there. "I know this sounds crazy, but it's what we have to do to save him."

"Do you know how many people have tried to kidnap, imprison, and kill Alataris over the years? Yet no one has succeeded. There's a reason for that, love." Grayson shoved his hands into his hair. He looked just as worn as I felt. His skin was paler than normal, and dark circles hung under his eyes. When I looked at the rest of the crew, they were all in similar states of exhaustion. Maybe I wasn't the only one feeling desperate, but I was the only one with a soul mate on the line. A soul mate I refused to live without.

The doors to the infirmary flung wide-open and smacked into the wall. Cross strutted through them, looking like a badass model on a runway. With his midnight hair hitting his jawline, black leather pants, and white V-neck shirt, he looked like he belonged on the cover of a magazine and was the only one who didn't lose a wink of sleep.

"What are you doing here?" I wasn't mad that he showed up in the middle of our little meeting, but these plans had to remain secret. Cross was new to Evermore, and I wasn't sure I could trust him.

"Figured you could use my help." He shrugged and took a seat on the cot on the other side of the aisle. The midday sun shined in on him, making him look like a temptation come to life.

"No offense, but how can you help us?" I glanced around the room at the others, who wouldn't meet my eye. "What? What'd I say?"

Cross cleared his throat. "Again, you really need to learn about the family ties in Evermore."

Was that aimed at me? Did he know about my dear old dad? It was a secret I had to keep. If the others found out, they may never trust me. I felt the blood drain from my face. "What's that supposed to mean?"

He cleared his throat. "My father is Dario Malback."

"Is that supposed to mean something to me?" Again, I looked at the others for some kind of hint at what he was getting at. But I got nothing. "Seriously, people. Start talking. You all have been in this world for way longer than me. A little help."

Beckett cleared his throat. "Dario Malback is Alataris' right-hand man. There isn't one thing that Alataris does without Dario knowing about or being a part of it."

"Yeah, that's Dad for you." Cross' words echoed my thoughts about my own father. But I never knew my father, or grew up with him. Cross was literally raised by the man who helped my greatest enemy. When he continued looking at the ground, I could almost see him waiting for us to send him packing.

"Let me ask you this—"

"No, I am not part of his cause. No, I'm not as evil as he is. And no, I will not tell him what's going on here," he snapped at me, then held his chin higher, as though waiting for me to insult him and his family, but I was not one to talk.

"Um, okay. That wasn't what I was going to ask." I rose from the cot and grabbed up a swath of fabric from Tuck's bedside and ran it across his forehead, dabbing away his fever. When I glanced up, Cross' jaw dropped.

"Okay, what were you going to ask me?"

"Why does your father support m—" I nearly said *mine*. "Alataris?"

Cross' brow furrowed. "Oh, um, I think because he's from an old-school way of thinking. You know, warlocks traditionally think those of us who have magic in our blood are superior in some way." He lowered his voice. "They lean toward dark magic to get what they want."

"So why would you help us? I'm not saying I don't trust you." I didn't. "Or that you'll betray us." He might. "But why would you help us with your dad and Alataris?"

His gold eyes met mine, and I swore I could see

myself in them. "Because, Zin, some of us can't choose who our parents are, can we?"

In that moment, I knew two things. First, Cross Malback knew exactly who my father was, and second, I couldn't trust him worth a damn, but he was all I had. "In that case, what do you suggest we do?"

"Grab my father instead. He'll be much easier to take, and he'll know the hex for sure." He crossed his arms over his chest, looking as confident as ever.

Nova stepped between us. "You can't be serious. Kidnap Alataris' right-hand guy? Are you people out of your minds?"

I shook my head. I honestly saw her point, but . . . "Desperate times call for desperate measures." I dabbed at Tuck's head once more before I dropped the rag and took my seat next to him. I turned back to Cross. "If you were going to grab him, then how would you do it?"

"I'd take him at the black market. He goes every Tuesday evening, and today just happens to be Tuesday." He shrugged.

This could be a trap. We could all fall to Alataris tonight because of Cross. But it was a chance I wanted to take. "Where's the black market?"

"Zin, you can't be serious." Grayson stood straight and buttoned his jacket. "This could go wrong in so many ways, love. Are you sure it's worth the try?"

"Is it worth the try?" My blood boiled in my veins. "I don't see any of us coming up with a better idea. Do you? Look at him, Gray. Just look!" I motioned to where Tucker lay unconscious and fighting for every breath he took. His cheeks were hollow, and his lips were as pale as his skin. "We have no time left. It's now or never."

Cross rose from his spot on his cot. "Beckett knows where the market is, don't you, Becks?"

All eyes swung toward him, and he narrowed his gaze at Cross. "I'm sure I can find it just fine."

When Cross turned for the door, I called out after him. "Wait. How will we know where to find him?"

"There's a specific herb my dad is looking for, and there's only one guy who will have it. Ali Chantra. You'll see his stand when you get there." He spun around and headed for the door.

"Hey, Cross, why are you helping us get your dad?" I had to know.

"Let's just say the pretty blonde he'll be with is not my mom. He's got it coming to him." Before I could ask him anything else, he disappeared behind the doors.

I jumped to my feet and marched out behind him. "Okay, people. We are doing this. If you're in, I'll meet you in the basement. If you're out, stay here and watch Tuck. It's time to save our leader."

CHAPTER 11

ZINNIA

The black market was anything but black. I expected shady knife-wielding characters in dark tents covered in masks . . . I was wrong. The market was unlike anything I'd ever seen before. It rose up in the middle of the desert and was completely hidden from the human eye. But the architecture was as old as any I'd ever seen in pictures of the Middle East. Each building held an array of browns that camouflaged with the surrounding desert. The limestone and mud structures formed a large main avenue, with tents and awnings in a rainbow of brightness.

Baskets of herbs and brightly-colored crystals lined the streets. Animals I'd never seen in the human world rattled about in cages. Something hissed at me as I passed its cage, baring its razor-sharp teeth at me. I leaned in closer, and a small lizard with an umbrella for a neck ran at the thin wooden bars and slammed its face into them. Then it scurried back. "Hey there, little guy."

"Zinnia." Nova wrapped her hand around my arm and yanked me back.

"Wha—" Just then, a ball of fire exploded out of the cage. The heat licked at my face as the small pillow of fire floated up and out of view. "Wow, thanks?"

Nova tucked her hair behind her ear. "No problem."

I knew I'd been a wild card lately, but I couldn't stop myself. Tuck was all that mattered. But through this whole thing, Nova had been by my side, a silent comforting presence I needed. She'd even given me the right clothing I needed to blend in here. The colorful sari fell from my hips to the ground. When I'd originally put the soft dress on, I didn't think I'd blend in, and bright yellow wasn't my color. But the red beads that adorned the hem of my skirt covered my combat boots perfectly, and only some of my stomach showed below the crop top. Stick-on jewels lined my eyebrows and the corners of my eyes. "Remind me again why we have to wear this."

Nova turned in her normal black Goth clothing for a violet sari that covered her from head to toe, including her white-blond hair. "Because if we show up here in our normal clothes, they'll know something is up with teenagers in leather leggings and combat boots. This place caters to all types of magical people, but for where we are going, we either need to blend in with the locals or embrace our darker sides and warlock ourselves up. I opted for locals. It's less intimidating."

"Ah, but what about your gloves?" I motioned to them.

She shrugged. "It works. What can I say?"

It didn't work, but I wasn't going to say anything else. At some point, she would tell me her secrets. "Where's everyone else?"

Her dark eyes darted upward. "Exactly where they're supposed to be. Beckett and Grayson are watching from the rooftops. Serrina and Tabi are just behind us, and Brax is up ahead."

I didn't dare look at any of them. I closed my eyes for a brief second and could feel all their powers around me. The colors of their magic danced behind my eyes. Nova's purple, Serrina's red, and Tabi's yellow. Even Adrienne, our substitute queen, had a faint blue glow. The guardians were a whole other old energy I didn't understand but felt all the same. "Where is this place at?"

"Beckett said we would know it by the big purple awning with a golden ring of fire embroidered into it."

I scanned the busy streets, looking at each tent, every piece of fabric I could lay my eyes on. Under my sari, my body quaked with nerves. This was our last chance. How many more times would I get to save Tuck's life? This was it. It had to work.

Nova pressed her hand to my arm. "This will work."

I couldn't say for sure that it would. When I turned back toward the end of the street, there stood a small flag with a tiny flaming circle embroidered into it and an arrow pointing down a dark alley. *Of course it's down a dark alley.* I stepped forward. "Come on. This way."

Nova moved to my side as we turned in the direction the arrow pointed. I threw my shoulders back and held my head high. No warlock would show fear to walk in here, and I wouldn't either. The buildings rose up so high they blocked the scorching sun and cast us into shadows. The vibrancy of the main street was all but forgotten. Beggars huddled on the ground, while small broken-down tables held objects I felt held the darkest of magic. I wrapped my hand around Nova's elbow and pulled her next to me. "There at the end."

I wanted this tent to be bright violet with golden symbols. What I got was dingy scrap of fabric with a faded gold ripped circle on it. The merchant behind the wooden planked table barely glanced up from the onyx stone he was polishing in his hand. "What do you want?"

His Middle Eastern accent was thick and rolling. The way he spat his words at me made me feel as though I was more an ant under his shoe than a paying customer. At five-foot-eight, he only stood five inches taller than me, though his paunch of a stomach hung well over his waistline, giving him at least seventy-five pounds extra over me. I pulled the picture of the orchid I'd ripped from the book out from between the folds of my dress. "I seek the seeds of this flower." I tossed the paper out onto the countertop.

The man rolled his eyes and sighed before he grabbed it up then flattened it out. He took one look at the paper and rolled his beady little eyes. "Don't have it."

"Look again," I spoke through gritted teeth. If this scum had the flower then we could avoid going after Dario altogether. If not, then we would have to proceed as planned.

He held the picture up, glanced at it, then crumpled it up into a ball and used it to wipe the sweat from his oily round face. "Go away, little girl. I have no time for games."

Proceed as planned it is.

Another smaller person came up beside us. Judging from how small they were, I thought it was a woman, but I couldn't tell. She was covered from head to toe with a black mask, dark black pants, and a black shirt hanging loose on her body. A large sword stuck out from the holder around her tiny waist.

He turned his attention toward her. "Can I help you?"

She gave me a sideways glance, then answered, "I need twenty death caps."

"Any size? Color?" He smiled at her. He actually smiled. All this time, he'd given us not even a glance.

"Surprise me." She reached across the table and snatched a crystal from a small sack on the table and tossed it up in the air and caught it. "This too."

He inclined his head toward her in a bow of respect. "Anything for you."

No time for games. That was it! Rage flooded my veins hot and heavy. I shoved the smaller woman to the side and leapt over the table, drawing my blade. I shoved the merchant through the flaps of his tent and up against the wall. I pressed my blade to his throat, nicking his skin enough so his blood would drip onto the sharp edge. "I'm so glad I got your attention now."

Nova shoved into the tent behind me. "Drop your sword!"

"What?" I shoved into him harder. "I'm not letting him go."

"Not you, him." She moved right next to me and yanked a sword from his hand, a sword I hadn't seen.

I wanted to pull the blade across his skin to punish him. Instead, I let my magic slither over my body in swirling streams of silver that wound down my arm toward the weapon I pressed to his neck. My magic turned into thick bands. In my mind, I saw them as two cobras ready to strike. Then it formed into exactly what I wanted. Silver metallic cobra heads lifted up off my arm and stopped inches from his face.

Their mouths hung open, and a low hiss erupted from each of them. The man held his hands up. "I tell the truth. I have no orchid poppy seeds."

"Good thing that's not what we're here for." I let my magical snakes slide from my arms and around his neck.

"What do you want?" His eyes bulged from his head.

"Dario Malback will be here at any moment. I want him."

The merchant shook his head back and forth. "If I do that, I die."

Nova shoved in beside me and pulled one of her gloves off. Her fingers hovered over his cheek, and her voice went low, hypnotic, threating. "Imagine if you will, knowing exactly how you're going to die. But never knowing when. Living your whole life running from death, knowing you can't change the way it's going to happen. Will you die an old man in a bed surrounded by family, or will your"—she glanced around the dark tent —"your shady dealings finally catch up to you? One touch. With only one touch, your fate will be sealed."

He whimpered but pressed his lips together.

"Hold him still. This is going to hurt. And after that, I hope it doesn't drive you to madness." She rose up on her tiptoes and stared him in the eye. "Because it has all those who have come before you."

The flaps to the tent flew open, and Beckett shoved his way through. "What are you two doing?"

"Getting results," Nova snapped back at him.

"This isn't how we do things." He reached out toward Nova, about to grab her hand.

"Don't touch her!" I kicked my leg back just enough to block him from touching her. Beckett held his hands out in surrender. I glanced over my shoulder at him. "Trust me, you don't want to."

The merchant leaned away from Nova, but my magical snakes pulled him back toward her. He turned his head away. "What do I have to do?"

A slow smile spread across my lips. "All you have to do is bring him back here. Leave the rest to us."

He closed his eyes and sighed. "Deal."

CHAPTER 12

"This is going to work. I know it." I crossed my arms and leaned back up against the wall in the back of the tent. If the tent hadn't been pushed up against a building, I would've fallen right through. Each wall was covered by the faded purple fabric. A threadbare carpet barely covered the hard-packed dirt floor.

Zinnia paced back and forth. "I need this to work."

"I know you do. And I think this will." I wanted to reassure her, to promise everything would be okay. But I didn't know if it would be.

She looked down at my gloves and back up at my face. "Is that why you wear the gloves? So you don't see people's deaths?"

It wasn't something I liked to talk about now or ever,

but she'd seen me do it, and I couldn't not answer her. "Yeah."

"How does it work?" She stopped pacing and leaned up against the wall next to me. "Like, how did it start?"

"It started when I was a little kid. First with my pets. I'd pet them and then I could see it so clearly how they would die, and no matter how hard I tried to change it, death would always come for them." I didn't want to cry. Not now, not ever. But I had cried for every single death I couldn't prevent.

Zinnia rested her hand on my shoulder. "I'm sorry you had to go through that."

"We all have our burdens to bear."

"Is it only in your hands, or is it all over?" She slowly lifted her hand from my shoulder. It was a reaction I'd grown so used to. People didn't want to know about their death. I understood that. If they knew how they would die, then their lives would be consumed with a way to try and stop it.

I nodded. "Only on my hands, the front and back. I guess that's kind of a blessing, huh?"

Zinnia threw her arm over my shoulder. "Well, I'm not scared of you, so there's that."

I didn't think she'd be so easygoing about it. I leaned into her and bumped her with my hip. "At least now you know I can threaten people with the best of them. I mean, magical cobras were pretty badass too."

She shrugged. "Nah, it was you who threw him over the edge." She lifted her arm and moved to the tent flap. "Do you think Beckett will forgive us?"

"I think Beckett has his own set of secrets to keep and ours are nothing compared to this. It's true what you said. We all have our things."

Zinnia waved her hand behind her. "He's coming." She peeked over her shoulder at me. "And you should see his mistress. She looks like a bleach blond Playboy playmate from the eighties. Huge blond hair. I mean, *huge*. And let's just say her chest matches the hair."

She dropped the flap and took a few steps back. "When he comes in, I'll have to drain as much of his power as possible. Then you do your thing, okay?"

I pulled my swords from beneath my skirts and held them loose at my sides. "I'm ready."

Zinnia stood as still as stone with her magic swirling around her. Her wild midnight locks crackled with power. My own rose to match hers, and purple sparks flew from my fingertips. Two queens ready to take down the right hand of an evil king. What could go wrong?

CHAPTER 13

ZINNIA

My magic pulsed around my body. It was ramped up by my uncontrollable nerves. Outside the tent, I watched as Dario beamed and cooed at his mistress. I could see why Cross wouldn't mind us capturing his father for a while. She was slightly smaller than him but only by an inch or two. What she lacked in height her hair made up for. A tight corset synched her waist in and pushed her breasts up to the point of almost choking her. Red velvet pants encased her legs like sausages. Each time he presented her with some gem or crystal, she giggled and nodded, and he would dump them into her purse.

I motioned for Nova to come up beside me. "Look at this."

Nova grabbed a corner of the tent and peeked through. "He's spending a small fortune on her."

"I'm guessing he has it to spend." I rolled my eyes. Dario Malback was exactly how I remembered him. His long black hair fell back from a widow's peak at the top of his head all the way below the middle of his back. A leather cord bound his hair at the nape of his neck. Though he wore a black leather jacket, it was styled like a suit coat, which seemed like a contradiction to me, and even worse were the matching pants.

The merchant motioned for Dario to follow him into the tent. "If you'll just follow me this way, sir. I have the herbs you ordered the last time you were here."

"Oh, Dari, I don't want to go back there and look at weeds. Can't you send someone to fetch it for you?" His mistress tugged on his arm, pulling him in the opposite direction.

He shook his head. "Some things need to be dealt with personally."

She tugged him even harder, pulling him off balance. Yet he leaned away from her.

I pulled the tent flaps closed. "Any minute now."

Nova nodded and held her swords at the ready. She looked like an epic assassin waiting for her next kill, with her sari hanging off her body. Her onyx eyes were laser focused, and her swords were polished and well cared for. Yes, she was the queen of the death cast, but right now she looked as though that's what she dealt with twenty-four seven.

Outside, the sound of raised voices drew my attention toward the flap. A moment later, Dario's mistress came tumbling through. She fell backward, taking the tent flaps with her. I stood frozen, my eyes locked on Dario's. All around, people stopped and stared at the falling tent, the messed-up table, and me standing with my magic swirling around me.

Dario growled, "You."

"Dari, who is this? Huh?" His mistress whined at my feet.

I didn't know if she was a witch or some other kind of super, but I didn't have time to find out. The words rushed from my mouth. "Moon above shine bright and take her mind to the middle of the night. Relax your mind and let your body flow free until the moment I wake thee."

Her body fell limply onto the threadbare carpet. "Watch her!" I barked at Nova before I took off after Dario. He spun around and ran for the main street.

Beckett dropped down beside me and kept pace as we chased after Dario. Above, I saw Grayson and Brax leaping from one roof to the next. Serrina and Tabi followed behind us. We all raced to capture the one man who was our last hope at saving Tuck. I pumped my arms harder and threw a ball of my magic at him. Dario zigged to the side. The ball missed him by inches.

"You're going to kill him," Beckett snapped at me.

"No, I'm not." I sucked in deep breaths as I sprinted to catch up.

Dario knocked over baskets full of powders and stones. They flew at me like missiles. Still, I didn't stop. Dust burned my eyes, and I stumbled over those tiny pebbles. But if I gave up now, there would be nothing left for Tuck. Up ahead, I could see a gap between the buildings. The sun shinned down on it like a finish line I had to reach as he did. I could feel the magic thickening as we got closer.

"What's that?" Beckett glanced toward me.

"I don't know, but we have to get there before he does."

Beckett threw a blue orb a few feet ahead of us, then grabbed my hand and pulled me toward the portal. "This way."

I didn't hesitate. I ran headlong for it. My body was pulled and twisted in all different directions. I thought for a second I would be torn apart, and then suddenly, I was put back together. Out we popped in that opening between the buildings. I spun in a circle, looking for Dario, when he skidded to a halt right in front of me.

"What do you want?"

I canted my head to the side. "Oh, Dari, isn't it obvious?" I narrowed my eyes at him and let my magic flow down my arms. "I want you."

He stumbled back and held his hand out in front of him while shaking his head. "No, you can't."

"But I can. And I will." I raised my hands above my head, ready to take his magic. I launched my streams of silver toward him. They wrapped around his body, and I felt the pull of his magic. It was so dark, so thick. A heavy copper taste filled my mouth. *Blood?* He gritted his teeth and held on to his powers, cocooning them around his body. Electric waves pulsed through my body, and I felt my feet lifting up off the ground. My hair stood on end, and I fought to take what he had.

I needed Dario. I couldn't fail. I wouldn't. I hovered a few feet off the ground. My muscles shook with the effort I was using to fight him for his powers. A bellow ripped from his throat, and he fell to one knee.

"Zin, you'll kill him!" Beckett screamed from somewhere nearby.

"No, I won't." I knew I wouldn't kill Dario, and the one and only reason why I wouldn't was because I needed him to save Tuck. Nothing else mattered.

Vivid orange light cracked from the wall behind

Dario. It flared out in a bright array like looking at the sun. Beckett ran headlong at Dario. "Now or never."

Grayson and Brax dropped in beside him. Ashryn, the noble elf and the one person I hadn't seen the whole time we were here, melted from the shadows. Her entire outfit was the color of sand, and she had her long sandy hair braided down the side of her body. She pulled two small daggers from the holsters on her thighs. As one, they charged toward him while I held him with my magic. The fissure in the wall behind him cracked wide-open, and fifteen Thralls spilled out around him. They wore black from head to toe with neon green accents and their black sunglasses. Five more warlocks flowed out behind them.

"Shit." My feet touched down on the ground just as Beckett, along with the other guardians, skidded to a halt. We were outnumbered and outmanned. I pulled my magic back in, letting Dario go for only a moment. "Surrender now and no one has to die here today."

"I was going to tell you the same thing." Dario rose to his feet and rolled his shoulders.

Serrina and Tabi slid in beside me. Red smoke drifted from Serrina's hands toward the warlocks beside Dario. She pursed her blood-red lips into a kiss and blew across the palm of her hand, sending it drifting over the ground toward them. Her streaked blond hair bounced with each of her movements. Her voice went low, lulling, tempting, and beckoning to them. "You want to come to me."

The warlocks closest to Dario took a step toward us. Dario held his hands up. "No, don't."

They hesitated at his command, but Serrina doubled the amount of smoke coming from her hands. "Dario, take a step toward me."

The Queen of Temptation wielded her power and bent his will. The fissure crackled and more light poured through. Then Alataris ducked his head through the hole and chuckled. "Dario, it appears you need some assistance."

"Alataris," I growled. I wanted to leap forward and rip him all the way out of that fissure.

He said nothing. Instead, he reached his hand out toward Dario. "Today is not the day for this. They have no hope for the future."

Dario didn't hesitate. He grabbed Alataris' hand and followed him back through the portal. Like a receding tide, the others flowed back into the hole.

"No! Not this time." I ran to follow him, to dive through that portal after him. A heavy arm wrapped around my waist, holding me back and stopping me in my tracks.

"Stop, Zin! You'll get us all killed." Beckett tightened his arms around me, holding me back.

I slung my arms and legs forward, fighting to get to Alataris. As the crack in the wall began to close, the last thing I saw was Alataris' smiling face. The fight left my body, and I sagged against Beckett.

He pulled me in closer, hugging me. "It's okay. We'll find another way. I know we will."

I shoved him away. "That's it! There is no other way!"

I turned from him, not knowing where I was going or what I would do, but I marched down those streets. People scurried out of my way, yet I couldn't think. I'd lost Tuck again, and this time it would cost him his life. I knew it. My breaths came in panicked puffs as I found myself back where it all began. Back in that merchant tent.

Nova stood over Dario's mistress with her swords still at the ready. When she took one look at me, she dropped them. "What happened?"

"We . . . um . . . we lost him." My words were halted and hurt each time I said one. I wasn't talking about Dario. I was talking about my soul mate . . .

Nova launched herself at me and wrapped her arms around my shoulders, pulling me in tight to her. "It'll be all right. We'll figure this out. Let's just wake up the bimbo and get back to school to Niche. There has to be something else."

As I looked down at that big hair, I froze. "No."

Nova let her arms slide away from me as she looked up at me. "No?"

"Take her with us. She might be useful after all."

CHAPTER 14

ZINNIA

"We aren't Alataris. We don't take hostages!" Beckett paced back and forth in the one room in the world where none of our magic would work . . . the detention room in Evermore Academy. The walls were a nondescript beige with a single window. The floor where the mistress lay was cold hard linoleum. The kind of linoleum you found in a public restroom. This was the only room in Evermore Academy that didn't look like an ancient castle and I wondered why they went to the trouble of updating it. Was it part of the non-magic enchantment or was it simply a late addition? Light rectangular oak tables lined the room. Each one had a single chair at it facing the wall. *Serious detention room. You can't even look at someone else?*

The others had gone off to either clean up or find

Niche, leaving only Grayson, Nova, Beckett, and myself to stand watch over Dario's still sleeping mistress. "She isn't a hostage."

He threw his arms up. "Oh no? Then what is she? Because from where I'm standing, that's exactly what she is."

By the time we got back to the school, it was the middle of the night and everyone was sleeping. The moon was full and round, shining through the window and illuminating the room in nighttime blues. It tinted Beckett's blond hair a light shade of violet, which he now jabbed his hands through.

I stood over her. "She's just a bargaining chip. If Dario finds out that we have her, he might—"

"Might what? Turn himself over to free the woman he loves?" Beckett motioned toward her sleeping on the floor. Her blond hair fanned out around her and even in sleep her face looked like it was glowing because of the amount of makeup she wore. "News flash: men don't love their mistresses, Zinnia. They keep them for one reason and one reason only."

I pressed my lips together, wanting to fight against every word he said. "You don't know that!"

"What the hell is going on here?" Matteaus shoved through the door, slamming it against the wall. It bounced off the wall, leaving a dent behind it.

My jaw dropped open. How could he have known we were here in this room? I glanced at Nova then Grayson, who both shared my jaw-dropping shock.

Matteaus crossed his arms over his chest. "Don't act so surprised to see me. This is my school and I know everything." His stormy eyes swirled with knowledge and power. Then moved down to the floor where Dario's mistress was. The muscle in his jaw flexed as he ground his teeth and muttered, "Kids, who decided I should work with kids?" He looked up toward the ceiling and clutched his hand into a fist as he shook his head.

I shuffled from one foot to the other. How was I going to explain kidnapping a woman and holding her prisoner in the detention room of my school? *I might get expelled for this one.* "W-we need her to help find a cure for Tuck's hex."

As he met my eye, he sucked in a deep breath and huffed it out. His wings ruffled behind him. "Do you have any idea what you've brought into this school?"

"I know it's Dario Malback's mistress, but I promise we will get rid of her as soon as we can. I just need to find a way to get the spell they have over Tuck, and she is our only option." I wanted to pace from one end of the classroom to the other, but I held still, forcing myself not to show an ounce of the nerves I felt. Awkward silence hung in the air as he looked from me at the woman and back again.

Matteaus rolled his eyes. "You know nothing." He waved his hand over the still sleeping mistress. The air around her wavered as though she was lying under water. Her blond hair began to melt away to long straight black tendrils. That overly tan skin faded to a snowy pale, and her clothing went from barely there to a thick gray sweater dress and black leggings.

I sucked in a sharp breath and shoved back from the girl sleeping on the ground. This wasn't Dario's mistress. This was an even bigger bargaining chip than I could imagine. A thrill of terror and excitement went through me. "Ophelia!"

Matteaus jabbed a finger in Ophelia's direction. "She can't stay here. You need to take her back to wherever you got her from." He didn't wait for me to say anything else. He turned around, muttering under his breath, "Build a school, they said. It'll be good for all the kids, they said. No one ever mentions the kidnappings . . ." When he turned for the door, black feathers fluttered to the ground behind him. Then he slammed the door so hard the wall shook.

Ophelia lay at my feet with her curtain of straight black hair fanned out around her. The light of the moon gave her skin an ethereal blue tint.

Grayson raced from the back of the room to perch on the teacher's desk in the front of the room. He looked down at her with wide, round chocolate eyes. "Oh, now you've gone and done it. You kidnapped Alataris' bloody daughter."

I am Alataris' daughter, I wanted to yell back at him, but I didn't. "It's not like she was our target. How were we supposed to know it was her the whole time?"

Nova crouched down beside Ophelia. "You know, when she sleeps, she doesn't seem that terrifying. Should we tie her up and drop her off a cliff or something?"

"Nova!" Even though Ophelia was as evil as Alataris, she was my sister, and a small fraction of protectiveness overcame me. *Like the smallest fraction ever.*

She shrugged. "I was joking. Well, kind of. But not really. No, I was joking."

I rolled my eyes. "We aren't going to hurt her."

"Then what are you going to do with her?" Nova came to stand in front of me. "We can't hold someone like her. We're all queens, and we all have a huge amount of power. But this girl, she's dangerous and unpredictable. Not to mention she's the daughter of our sworn enemy. She can't be trusted."

I hesitated. Would they all feel this way about me once they found out I was her half-sister? Would they want to toss me out too? I had his blood running in my veins. I was a Queen Siphon Witch and he was an evil siphon warlock king. If anything, they should worry about me. I wanted to defend her parentage, but who was I to say anything? I couldn't.

"Who her parents are has nothing to do with who she is," Beckett growled. "It's her choice to be who she is."

"Hold up." I raised my hand to cut them all off. "This is a castle, right? There has to be a dungeon somewhere."

Grayson, Beckett, and Nova all shared nervous looks, yet none of them spoke. I didn't have time for this. We needed answers, and we needed them now. Tuck's life depended on it. "What?"

"Matteaus said to get rid of her, Zin. We can't just hold her hostage here." Grayson tiptoed around her like she was a snake about to strike.

"Look, this might be the only chance we get to find something to help Tuck, and I don't know about you guys, but I think we owe it to him to try anything." I looked down at her. "And I mean anything. Are you with me?"

Before I even looked up, Nova moved to stand at my side. "I'm with you."

I smiled at her and turned toward Beckett. "Becks?"

He rolled his head on his shoulders and sighed. "Yeah, I'm with you."

"Gray?"

"As your former fake boyfriend, how could I deny you?" A grin spread across his face, and he moved to stand over Ophelia. "Off to the dungeon with her then."

I crossed my arms over my chest. "Lock her up, boys."

CHAPTER 15

I'd gone from average teenager, to a queen witch, to an official kidnapper. The worst part about it was . . . I didn't care. In a hidden basement of Evermore Academy, I stood in front of thick metal bars that were jabbed into the heavy stones, holding them in place. The only light in the cell was the blue moonlight drifting in from the small rectangular window.

I slowly paced back and forth in front of the bars, debating on what I would do or say. Grayson and Nova left us the moment the door slid shut on Ophelia's cell. Beckett stood just outside the room, standing guard. Though I could only see the back of his shoulder I could tell his back was stiff and unmoving. Maybe I wasn't the only one nervous about what we were doing. My boots scraped against the stones with each step I took, and the damp basement smell invaded my nose. I pulled my hoodie tighter around my body. I didn't know what I was going to do with her or what to offer her in exchange for the information I needed.

"Are you freaking kidding me?"

I startled and turned toward the deep voice rumbling behind me. "Headmaster Matteaus."

He melted from the shadows behind me. I knew it was impossible, but he seemed bigger in this small space. He towered over me, and his biceps were the size of my head. He put his hands on his hips and leaned back against the wall. "We aren't in the habit of keep teenagers prisoner in this school, Miss Heart."

"I know that. But I honestly couldn't think of anything else to do." I held my breath, waiting for him to yell at me, waiting for my expulsion.

He closed his eyes and let his head fall against the wall. "Zinnia, this school is here to teach you how to use your powers. What you choose to do with them is up to you. Whether you embrace your darker side or not is up to you." His gaze bore into mine. Did he know who my father was? Did he know I was willing to go as dark as I had to in order to save Tuck?

"I have no intention of embracing my dark side here. I just want to find out what she knows so I can help Tucker. That's it."

"She isn't lying." Another man larger than Matteaus marched through the doorway of the jail. He stood a few inches taller than Matteaus, with wavy black hair that fell just past his shoulders. Three days' worth of stubble covered his strong angular jaw, and a jagged scar ran through his eyebrow. When he looked at me with swirling emerald eyes, I felt like he was reading my soul. Oversized black wings peeked over his shoulders. Each feather was dark as night and ended in a vivid purple. In my mind, I immediately pictured him on the back of a huge Harley with shitkickers on and a leather vest. A pair of noise-canceling headphones were wrapped around his neck.

"Zinnia, this is Aidenuli. Aidenuli, this is Zinnia, our resident kidnapper and hostage negotiator."

Aidenuli nodded at me. "Hi." He didn't smile or have an ounce of warmth behind his sharp eyes.

"I'm not a hostage negotiator. I just want to know how to save him. Do you really want a student to die under your watch?" I turned toward the bars and looked at Ophelia still under my spell. If it was up to me, I would leave her sleeping in peace until this thing with Alataris was over and done with. But I couldn't, not when Tuck's life depended on it. "I just need the cure to help him, and I'm determined to get it."

"What means are you going to use? She's not just

going to tell you what you want to know." He motioned to Ophelia.

I shrugged. "Well, I'm not going to hurt her, if that's what you're asking. Something tells me she'll negotiate for her freedom." I didn't know what made me think she wanted something from us, but my gut was telling me she would. Whether or not I could come through would be another story. I was in no position to strike a bargain and I wouldn't release her until I got what I wanted.

Matteaus shoved away from the wall and came to stand next me. "I'm only going to say this one time and one time only. You have twenty-four hours to figure this out. After that, I'm letting her go. No one wants to see anything happen to Tuck. Even I kind of like the guy."

I sucked in a sigh of relief. "I thought you were going to expel me."

He shook his head. "Nah. What's a little coercion between enemies to save a life?"

Magic school is so much cooler than public school. I beamed up at him. "I'll be good. I promise."

"Oh, I think you will be, and just in case you aren't, my guy Aidenuli over there is going to be standing watch. Trust me, if you even *think* about crossing a line, he will know it." He placed a hand on my shoulder and gave it a little squeeze, then walked out the door.

Aidenuli moved to a small wooden bench and let his

large frame drop down on it. I thought the bench was going to explode into pieces under his weight. Yet it didn't. He motioned to the cell. "Proceed." His voice was deep and rumbling.

I sucked in a deep breath and held my hands out, letting my magic flow over Ophelia. It floated over her body like a sparkling silver dome. "What lies asleep now must wake. By the power of the sun I give you energy to take. Open your eyes and rise with the moon. Open your eyes and greet us all in this room."

Ophelia didn't move a bit. She lay in the same position Grayson dropped her in. Yet her breaths were no longer deep and even. I glanced at Aidenuli. "Is she up?"

He gave the smallest of nods, telling me she was. I turned and kicked the bottom of the bar. The sound vibrated up the bar with a ting. I wrapped my hands around them so tight my knuckles turned white. "Wake up."

"Ugh, a girl needs her beauty rest, you know?" Ophelia sighed and rolled to her side.

"You're not fooling anyone, Ophelia. We know you're not Dario's mistress."

She sat straight up on the cot and looked down at herself. "Damn it!" She tossed her legs over the side of the bed and leapt to her feet. She swung her gaze around the room. Her opal eyes locked on the bars for a moment before landing on Aidenuli and then back on me. "Where am I?"

"You're in the dungeon in Evermore Academy, and I won't be letting you out until you give me the information I want." I backed away from the bars and crossed my arms, ready to wait her out for as long as it took.

Her gray sweater dress swallowed her tiny body, and her long black hair fell straight down to her waist. Black leggings clung to her thin legs, and a simple pair of black UGGs covered her feet. She looked so different than our first meeting when she'd taken a page out of Wednesday Addams' book. "I didn't think they kept prisoners in Evermore Academy."

I narrowed my eyes at her. "They made an exception just for you. For now. In a few more hours, who knows where they'll take you?"

Had she just swallowed? Was that a tremble I sensed in her hands? She took a step toward the bars. "And what exactly is it that you want?"

There was no use beating around the bush. With only twenty-four hours to get what I wanted out of her, I didn't have time to play games. "Your father hexed Tucker Brand, a very close friend of mine. I need to know how to break that hex. And you're going to tell me how to do it."

She arched an eyebrow at me. "*My* father? Don't you mean ours, sis?"

I could feel the blood draining from my face. "How did you—"

"There isn't much I don't know." She strolled up to the bars, standing only a foot away. "I wonder what the rest of your friends would think if they knew who you were exactly."

She was baiting me, trying to sway me from what I needed to know. She canted her head to the side, studying me with those obsidian eyes of hers.

I didn't turn away, didn't show any weakness. Instead, I placed my arms through the bars and rested them on the horizontal one running across the middle. "It doesn't matter. All that matters is getting Tuck better."

"And in exchange for what you want . . ." She studied her nails. "What do I get out of it?"

"Your freedom." I didn't want to let her go back out into the world to act as Alataris' general, but to save Tuck I would. Anything was on the table.

She tapped a finger to her lips. "And you say it's a hex our father put on him?"

"Ugh, he is not my father. And yes, can you help break the hex or not?"

Ophelia shook her head. "No one can break a hex

without knowing what it is first. But I can make it so that he'll be heathy enough to function until the hex reveals itself."

I leaned down and met her gaze. "What do you mean reveals itself?"

"Do they teach you nothing here?" She narrowed her eyes and pursed her lips as she gave Aidenuli a dirty look. "A hex of any short will eventually show itself. If the person who's hexed is supposed to die, then there will be signs leading up to it, for example."

I straightened my stance and took a small step back. What if the curse was meant to kill him slowly? I pressed my hand to my mouth, stifling a gasp. "You think he's cursed to die?"

She rolled her eyes. "No, it was an example. Don't be so dramatic. If he was cursed to die, he would be dead by now."

"So, you're saying you can help him?" I could hear the hope in my own voice, and I wanted to kick myself for letting her see it.

Ophelia leaned against the bars. "For a price, yes."

Am I striking a deal with the devil? Sure felt like it. "I already told you I'd let you go."

"I don't want to be let go." A smirk spread across her face. "I want to stay."

My jaw dropped wide-open and I froze.

"Don't act so surprised, Zin. Everyone has a secret they want."

It was true. Secretly I wanted for Tuck and me to be together without consequences. I shook my head, trying to fight against my disbelief. "You want to stay in this jail?"

"No! I want to be accepted at Evermore Academy. I want to go here. Make that happen and I'll save the little fire birdie who's captured your *special* attention." She backed away from the bars and plopped onto the cot. "Those are my terms."

"Let me get this straight. You want to be a student here? How do I even know you have the power to do what you'll say you can do for Tuck?" Was she messing with me? She wanted to stay? None of this made any sense. If it happened, would I be setting myself up for an even bigger mistake later on?

"Because I have this." She bent down and pulled a folded piece of paper from the side of her boot.

When she opened it up, I sucked in a sharp breath. "The orchid. How do you have it?"

"Doesn't matter how I have it. Only that I do. Do we have a deal? Can you get me into this place?" She held the flower out in front of her, taunting me with it. I wanted it more than I wanted anything. I was tempted to open the jail cell and rip the flower out of her hand.

As if sensing my desires, she folded the paper back up and shoved it into her boot. "And don't even think about stealing it. You wouldn't know what to do with it even if you did have it. Only I can make a potion strong enough to help your precious Tuck, and you know it."

"I don't know it. We have Niche and Professor Davis to help me make the potion."

Ophelia shook her head. "Neither of them is a queen of potions." She sat with her legs crossed. "Only I can make it exactly how strong and effective you need it. And what I'm asking in return is to go to school here. So, make it happen."

I threw my arms up, then turned toward Aidenuli. "Is it even possible?"

He looked from Ophelia back at me, then rose to his full towering height. "I'll see what I can do," was all he said before he left us alone together.

Suspicion riddled my mind. *It can't be this easy.* "If you betray me and something happens to Tuck, I will make you regret it." My fingers twitched with the need to summon my blades to make my threat seem more real, but I didn't trust myself not to get carried away. *Desperate times, desperate measures?*

"I have no doubt that you will. We share the same blood, after all, and holding a grudge is a specialty in our family."

"What family? Just because your creep of a father donated some swimmers to my mom sixteen years ago doesn't make us a family. It makes us people who share the unfortunate coincidence of having the same DNA. Nothing more." I began pacing back and forth in front of her cell. I couldn't believe I was actually considering trying to get her into the school.

"Whatever you say, big sis." Ophelia pulled the paper from her boot once more and waved the flower back and forth continually as we waited for Aidenuli's return.

What seemed like an eternity later, he walked back into the room and sat down. "It's done."

Ophelia popped up from her cot and sauntered over to the cell door. "Damn, sis, you got some pull in this place or what?"

When she reached for the door, I placed my hand over it, holding it closed. "You can come out on two conditions."

She put her hand on her hip and began tapping her foot. "Your little boyfriend doesn't have much more time. So you better tell them to enroll me real quick."

"One, if this doesn't work, you have to leave and go back to Alataris."

She nodded in agreement. "And number two?"

"No one, and I mean no one, not even Tuck, can know we are related. The fact my father is who he is will remain a secret until I'm ready for it to come out. Got it?"

"Boy, you must really trust your friends if you want to keep this from them." She tossed her hair over her shoulder as she rolled her eyes.

My heart raced with the need to get the potion to Tuck. But if Ophelia was going to stay, things needed to be handled. "Do we have a deal or not?"

Ophelia let out a long sigh. "We have a deal. If I didn't know any better, I'd think you wouldn't want anyone to know you're my big sister." Sarcasm dripped from each word she spoke.

I took a step back from the bars. "The question is, why would I want people to know about something I myself am ashamed to admit?" Before she could say anything else to piss me off, I turned away from her and marched out the door to go and save my forbidden soul mate.

CHAPTER 16

NOVA

"I can't believe you actually agreed to this." I sat perched on the edge of one of the long lab tables in the potions room. At this time of night, the stools in the classroom were all turned upside down and sitting on top of the tables. At the front of the room Ophelia, one of my sworn enemies, stood with a cauldron in front of her. The flame burned low underneath it, causing a constant bubble and boil. Steam rose up from it, and a floral scent wafted over me.

"What else can I do? I had to save Tuck. There was no other choice." Zinnia stood next to her, watching every single drop of content that went into that cauldron. Yet being a new queen, she didn't know what was going in there, but I did.

"You know what we're dealing with here is black

magic? That's exactly what it is. All those ingredients combined together could take down an elephant, let alone a phoenix who is already fighting for his life." I gritted my teeth. "She can't be trusted."

Ophelia tossed in one of the small leaves of the orchid and a purple death cap mushroom that she stole from the professor's cabinet. "Hello, I'm standing right here and both of my ears work, thank you very much."

"I don't care if you can hear me or not. It's obvious you can't be trusted. Do you know how many times I faced off against you and your father's Thralls? How many people have died underneath his rule? Zinnia, you have to see this is crazy. It could kill him." I leaned forward and shoved my hands into my hair, tying it in a high topknot. Zinnia was my closest friend. I wanted to help her. I really did. But even this seemed a bit crazy to me.

"If you see another option here, then I'm open to listening to it. But as it is right now, this is our only option. Tuck has hours left, maybe even a few minutes. If we can save him now, I'm going to do it." She met my gaze, and I could see the determination in her sapphire eyes. Her face was usually so bright and full of life but was now cold and determined.

I motioned toward the cauldron and the contents on the table. "We don't know if she's going to save him.

This could kill him, Zinnia. Are you ready for that? Are you ready to lose him?"

"Ugh, are all of you always so dramatic? I'm not gonna kill the little bird boy, okay? You want him to live, I'm going to make him live and in exchange I get to stay here." Rosie light drifted up from the cauldron, illuminating her pale face in hues of pink and purple. She grabbed up one of the vials and pulled the ladle free from the cauldron, dumping the contents into that vial.

I shook my head. "I don't trust this, and I don't trust you. Why would you want to stay here? All you've been fighting for your entire life is to keep us from stopping your dear old dad. She's a spy. I just know it, and there's nothing worse than being a snitch. I don't care if I am being unreasonable." She couldn't be trusted, and Zin knew it. She was so desperate to save Tuck that she believed there was no other way around this. Maybe there wasn't, but I wanted to avoid having to deal with Ophelia. My only hope was that if we kept her here, we would keep our enemies closer than our actual friends. I could watch her and make sure she wasn't out to hurt the rest of us. At least that's what I was telling myself as I watched her put a little cork in the top of that vial and hand it over to Zin's waiting hands.

"Nova, he's going to die without this potion. It is our only shot at me seeing those honey-colored eyes again.

I'm gonna do it. I'm going to give this to him, and when he wakes up, you'll see it'll all be worth it." Zinnia wrapped her hands around that vile as if it were a silent prayer to save her Tucker. But deep down I knew it couldn't be that easy. One little potion and he'd be fine? Nothing was ever fine when it came to Alataris and his daughter.

I pointed to my eyes, and then I pointed at Ophelia. "Just so you know, I'll be watching your every move. One little step, one little toe out of line, and I will take you out."

Ophelia snickered. "Take me out to where? Dinner? Come on, Goth Barbie. You and I both know you aren't killing anyone." She marched over to the door and waved Zinnia through it. "Come on, let's get the show on the road. I've got a class schedule to look at and boys to meet."

I rolled my eyes. "I think I liked her better when she was dressed like Wednesday Addams and only said a couple of words."

"Oh, don't worry, death girl. I'll grow on you. Only takes a little bit of time." Ophelia filed in behind Zinnia and me, following us down the hallway at school.

I kept pace with Zinnia as I muttered, "Yeah, grow on me like a flesh-eating fungus I can't get rid of."

"Ooh, I'm shaking in my boots." Though Ophelia was

smaller than both of us and very slight, she was tough as any other witch I'd ever met before.

Zinnia stopped in the middle of the hallway. "Will you two just stop for minute? Just stop! This is important. We need to make sure that Tuck is okay. And your bickering isn't helping. So, either shut it and come along or go back to your rooms and wait until you hear my news." She turned away from me and marched toward the infirmary. When one of the pixies flew into her face, Zinnia batted it away the same way she would a gnat.

I sucked in a deep breath and jogged to catch up to her. "Okay, I'll calm down. I'm here for you. Now let's go save our leader, shall we?"

CHAPTER 17

ZINNIA

"Get out of my way, Beckett." I held the vial in the palm of my hand, clutching it to me like it was a lifeline. Indeed, it was a lifeline, not just for me but for Tuck. The glowing pink potion was still warm in my grasp. I wanted to give it to him more than anything.

The rest of the crew was spread out around the infirmary. They were perched on cots and stood in a semicircle next to Tuck. Even Niche and Matteaus stood off to the side watching.

Beckett held his hand out in front of himself. "I can't let you do this."

Beams of the rising sun glistened in through the wall of windows, giving the already sterile white room a bleached-out shining effect. Each of the cots leading down to Tuck were made up in military style with all the sides tucked in, ready for the next patient. As it was now, he was the only one here. From where I stood just inside the double doors, I could see his breath had gone shallow and the sweat that used to mat his hair was all dried up. His auburn waves fell back from his face in a tangled wavy mess. His eyes darted behind his lids, but his body remained motionless.

I stepped up, ready to shove past Beckett and go to Tuck. "We don't have much time left. I'm giving this to him."

Grayson moved to stand next to Beckett. "No, you're not. Why would Ophelia help you now? This could all be a plan to kill our leader."

Ophelia huffed. "Right, because the smartest thing to do is make a potion that would kill Tucker and stay here in the school surrounded by his crew with no way of escaping. Yeah, that seems absolutely brilliant."

"Maybe you don't care if you get away or not," Grayson snapped back at her.

Ophelia rolled her eyes. "Easy there, baby vamp. I wouldn't want you to get all fangy with me." She crossed her arms over her chest. "And I'm not going to kill your precious leader. I have every intention of staying in this school, so him being alive is to *my* benefit."

"A selfish reason if I ever heard one." He put his

hands on his hips and moved a step closer to Beckett, as though forming a wall.

Kumi, who'd been quietly watching from where she lay on the floor, growled in Grayson's direction. *Can I bite him now?*

No, he's still on our side. I shook my head.

Come on, the vamp needs to know what it feels like to get bitten. She pulled her lips back from her teeth.

"No, Kumi." I stomped my foot. I had enough to deal with, let alone rogue giant mythological wolf-dog nine-tailed creatures.

She whimpered and put her head back on the floor. *You never let me have any fun.*

I turned toward Niche. "What do you have to say about this?"

Niche swallowed and pushed her glasses farther up her tiny nose. "It's a risk." She glanced over at Tuck. "But it's a risk I'd take."

Tuck's body shuddered, and he began choking. Foam dripped from the side of his mouth onto the pillow behind his head. Gasping breaths stuttered from his lips.

Ophelia shoved me in the back. "It's now or never."

I pushed forward, trying to shove by Beckett and Grayson. They wrapped their arms around me and held me back from him. I wanted to unleash my magic on them. I wanted to decimate anyone who stood between

Tuck and me. Panic tightened my chest and I threw my weight into trying to get by them. My heart raced and my hands shook as I watched him struggle just to breathe.

Brax moved in beside Beckett and Grayson. He placed his hand on my shoulder. "No, Zin. We can't do this."

I grabbed his wrist and tried to yank it from my shoulder, but trying to move a towering shifter was like trying to push a brick wall over. I shot a look at Ashryn, one of the other guardians. "Are you going to step in too?"

She leapt up onto a shelf close to the ceiling and crossed her legs. "I do not believe you are incorrect."

With my heart racing, I noticed the other queens stepping to the side and out of the way. "I'm sorry about this, guys."

I threw my hand out, and silver magic exploded outward like a shock wave. Brax, Beckett, and Grayson were knocked off their feet and sent flying in different directions around the room. Before they could make their way back to their feet, I rushed to Tuck's side.

Ophelia stood next to his head. With one hand she held his forehead down and with the other she forced his mouth open. "Every drop in."

I pulled the cork from the top of the vial and held it

over his open mouth. I hesitated. If I did this, I could kill him or save him.

Ophelia kicked the side of the cot. "Now, Zinnia, before he stops breathing."

I twisted my wrist to the side and dumped the liquid down his throat. Ophelia shoved his mouth closed and held it that way until his throat bobbed as he swallowed the contents down. She shoved away from him and took a few steps back.

I dropped to my knees beside his bed, waiting. "Please wake up, please."

His breaths quickened as dull pink light traveled through all his veins. The muscles in his body thrummed tight with tension, and his hands curled into fists. I wrapped my hand around his and pried his fingers open, then shoved my fingers between his. "It's going to be okay."

He tiled his head back and screamed so loud it pierced my ears.

I glared at Ophelia. "What's happening?"

"The potion is working. It has to burn the hex away somehow." She leaned up against the wall like she was watching a boring movie rather than Tuck struggling for his life. "It's gonna sting a bit."

Just as I thought I couldn't take any more, his body went limp and a shuddering breath rattled his chest. A small pink sparkling ball floated out of his mouth. It burned brighter, sending a blinding light all around the room. I pressed my face into the cot at his side, waiting for it to stop. I squeezed my eyes shut and said a silent prayer for him to be okay. I'd taken my only chance at saving him. I could only hope it didn't backfire. I held his hand as tight as I could.

His fingers clutched to mine, squeezing them. "Zinnia?" His voice was weak and hoarse. But hearing my name on his lips sent a jolt of excitement through me.

My head snapped up. "Oh my God, Tuck. Are you okay?"

He swallowed and nodded. "What happened?" He blinked slowly and struggled to move his head to look around the room.

"Shh, don't move around. You've been through a lot." Tears of relief steamed down my face and I quickly swiped them away.

A cup of water appeared next to my face. "Here, give him this." Ophelia handed me the glass with a bent straw in it. "He needs to hydrate after what he's been through."

I nodded up at her. "Thank you." I wanted to leap to my feet and hug her for what she'd done.

I grabbed the cup and brought the straw down to Tuck's lips. "You were hexed by Alataris. But you're going to be okay now. I promise. Thanks to Ophelia."

He pressed his hand to his head. "Did you just say Ophelia?"

"Believe it or not. She saved you." In that moment, I was glad it was her I'd accidentally kidnapped. Hell, at that exact second I was kind of happy she was my sister.

He shook his head. "I think I might be going crazy, Zin."

I leaned forward. Ophelia said the potion would wake him and let him live until the hex revealed itself. Was it revealing itself so soon? "I'm here. What do you mean you think you're going crazy?"

"I could've sworn you said Ophelia." He closed his eyes and sighed. "Must be losing it."

"Well, I can see I'm so wanted here, but I really must be going to my room now." Ophelia strode toward the double doors of the infirmary. Like the Red Sea, everyone parted for her to pass as she walked by. When she got to the doors, she paused and turned on her heels to look at Matteaus. "Where exactly is my room?"

A dark chuckle rumbled deep in his chest. "You're rooming with Zinnia. She made this happen, so she can watch you."

I knew something bad would come of this. I groaned and let my head fall onto the cot once more. "I knew it was too good to be true."

"Well, consider it a lifetime of missed babysitting all

rolled into one." She pushed the doors open and called over her shoulder. "See ya later, roomie."

Tucker reached his hand over toward me and ran his fingers through my hair. "Thank you for saving my life."

I wanted to say I'd do anything for him, the way I knew he'd do anything for me. But I didn't. "Anytime." When I looked up to meet his eyes, I hesitated. Those smoldering honey-colored eyes I'd grown so used to were now swirling pools of black. The mark around my wrist tightened uncomfortably. Was it the hex turning his eyes black? I didn't want to point it out to anyone. He'd already been through so much. Now wasn't the time to worry him. He needed to rest. He needed to recover. Whatever was happening to him we would figure out together.

Before I could say anything else, the doc pushed in next to Tuck with his stethoscope. He pressed it to his chest and then to his side. "You gave us quite the scare, Mr. Brand." Then he turned to the rest of us and motioned toward the door. "Now I really must insist you all leave and let him get his rest."

I didn't budge. This was Tucker and I was staying.

The doc ran his hand over his bald head. "Headmaster Matteaus, please. He needs to recuperate, and having all of them in here is quite inconvenient."

Tuck cleared his throat. "It's okay, guys. I'm tired

anyways. Go get some sleep." He squeezed my hand one last time. "You too, Zin. You need a little R and R."

I lumbered to my feet and dropped his hand. "Okay. I'll be back to see you in a couple of hours."

His eyes turned from black to honey and back again. "I'll be waiting."

As we all filed out the door, I was the last to leave. Kumi rose to her feet and began to trot out behind me. *I need you to stay. Something isn't right about him.*

He does smell weird. It could be black magic or that he hasn't showered for days. She chuckled in her mind.

I don't know, but please just watch him for one more night.

Consider it done.

CHAPTER 18

I curled my hand into a fist, then lifted it to knock on Zinnia's door. A whole day had passed since Tuck took the potion to help ease his hex, and Zinnia had yet to be seen. The hallway was packed full of other students rushing to get to their classes. Pixies zoomed overhead, carrying notes and gossiping with each other. Their white blond hair flew out in all different directions. On the other side of the door, I could hear her staggering around her room.

Then the door was yanked open and Zinnia clung to the doorframe looking completely disheveled. Her hair was wrapped up in a messy ponytail, and she wore only a black cami and baggy pajama pants that hung off her hips. "What is it? What's wrong? Is Tuck okay?"

Her eyes went wide with worry, and she stumbled

back from the door and moved to turn on all the lights in her room. Across from her bed sat another bed where Ophelia lay groaning.

"Ugh, seriously, don't you people ever sleep in?"

I stepped in from the noisy hall and closed the door behind me. "You guys have been sleeping for a whole day straight. It's the morning after you gave Tuck the potion and Headmaster Matteaus wants you both to attend classes today."

Zinnia froze and glanced up at me. "So, Tuck is okay?"

I nodded. "He's great. He's back to normal and going to class today."

A wide smile spread across her heart-shaped face and she went to the closet. An assortment of black clothes flew through the doorway. "I can't believe he's okay. This is amazing!"

"Volume, people. Volume." Ophelia slouched over in her bed and rubbed at her face. "It's morning. Everything should be quiet in the morning."

Zinnia stepped out of her closet in a pair of black jeans that were torn at the knees and up her thighs. She wore a black long-sleeved T-shirt to match, which also had specific holes cut into it so her white cami would show through. She topped it all off with a maroon scarf that made her pale skin and sapphire eyes pop. Her hair was still piled in a tangled mess of midnight waves with some pieces hanging down around her face. She held her arms out. "Do I look okay?"

"You look great. Ready for classes today?"

Ophelia grabbed something off the nightstand next to her and hurled it at Zinnia. "Use that and lover boy will be eating out of the palm of your hand."

Zinnia caught it, looked down at it, and then turned for the bathroom. Once she closed the door behind her, I narrowed my eyes at Ophelia. "You can't use love potions on other students."

Ophelia slumped back on the bed and threw her arm over her face. "Good thing it's not a potion. But a little— scratch that, a lot—of eyeliner would help make her eyes pop more."

"Oh." I adjusted my backpack on my shoulder. "Sorry."

"Did that hurt? To, you know, apologize to someone like me?" Ophelia threw her legs over the side of the bed and began pulling on the same clothes she'd worn the day before. "Maybe before you judge someone you should think about the situations they've been put in and what they did to survive to get through it all."

What could I say to that? Was Ophelia just truly trying to survive being in Alataris' world, or was she playing us all? I didn't have an answer. Instead, I pulled my backpack from my shoulder, unzipped it, and jerked out a piece of paper Matteaus ordered me to give her. "Here, I'm supposed to give you this."

Ophelia stomped over to me and grabbed the paper from my hand. "What is it?"

"Your class schedule."

Zinnia came out of the bathroom and stopped to look Ophelia up and down. "Hey, O."

O? Since when were they on such friendly terms? Ophelia and I turned in unison. "O?"

"Yeah, O." Zinnia walked over to her closet and opened the door. "Feel free to pick whatever you want, okay? Maybe we'll go out shopping and grab some stuff for you later."

Ophelia's jaw dropped, and she narrowed her eyes at Zinnia. "What's the catch?"

Zinnia glanced at me then back at her. "What do you mean catch?"

"Okay, fine. What do you want in exchange for sharing your clothes?" She put her hands on her hips and began tapping her foot.

"I don't get what you're asking." Zinnia began walking around their room and pulling books down from the dark wooden book shelves. She piled them on the edge of her desk and picked her backpack up off the floor. She yanked the zipper open and placed the bag on her chair.

Ophelia huffed. "Do you want like an endless supply of potions or something? Or do you want me to do your homework for you?"

Zinnia paused while shoving a book in her backpack. "Um, no. I'd prefer to do those on my own."

"Well, you have to do them on your own if you're going to be ready for your Magtrac exams. I mean, both of you have to get ready for them if I'm being honest." I moved to sit on the end of Zinnia's bed.

"Okay, first of all, O, you can borrow my clothes because I know you don't have any other than the ones on your back. Secondly, it's called being nice. You proved yourself to me last night, and I'm going to give you the benefit of the doubt until you prove me wrong—"

"But your friends—"

"My friends don't influence the way I think, so feel free to borrow whatever." Zinnia turned toward me. "Now you, what the hell are you talking about Magtrac exams?"

I shifted in my seat. "Oh, um, all students need to take the Magtrac exams within the first year they're here to determine which classes they'll be assigned for the duration of school. Not everyone is made to be a queen witch, you know?"

Ophelia snickered. "That's the damn truth." She walked past Zinnia and straight into the closet. "Why do you have so many clothes? It doesn't make sense."

"There's not that many." Zinnia looked taken aback when she looked at me. "I swear there's not that many."

"You're looking at the girl who has an extra rack in her room for more clothes. I am not one to judge." I held my hands up as if I was surrendering to my clothing problem.

"But really, though, when are these exams? I have to be ready. I mean, what if they send me on the wrong track?" She bit her bottom lip and started grabbing more books.

"Well, there are only two exams really. It's the practical magic exam to see how powerful you are and if you can control your magic. Then there's the hand-to-hand exam, as in combat." When she looked at me with wide eyes, a giggle escaped my lips. "Don't worry. You have like two weeks to get ready."

"Two weeks!" She raced around the room and grabbed her notebooks, then threw her backpack over her shoulder. "I feel like I've spent the last few weeks saving the world and battling an evil dude. Now I have to be a normal teenager and study to pass exams? What the hell?"

"Trust me, none of us are normal." Ophelia popped out of the closet in a black and red plaid coat with white faux fur around her collar, a black glittery tank top and red leggings. She held her hands up. "What do you think?"

Zinnia looked her up and down. "Where did you find red leggings?"

"At the bottom of all the black ones." Ophelia beamed. "I like them."

"Keep them." Zinnia motioned to the door. "You ready to go? We have to get to classes. Nova, what happens if I fail these exams?"

I knew she wouldn't fail, but I could see the doubt in her eyes. I shrugged, going for nonchalant. "Your classes will be changed to basic magic and how to blend in with the world around you. Not everyone is made to be a warrior or rule in Evermore. For the ones who aren't, they need to learn to use their powers in very average ways."

Ophelia grabbed an empty knitted hobo bag off the floor and threw it over her shoulder. "What do they call the different tracks? I mean, there's only two, right?"

"There's four. You're either on the citizen, apprentice, warrior, or advanced." I rose from the chair and followed them out the door.

Zinnia opened the door and stepped out into the corridor. "What track are you on?"

"Advanced."

"I'm guessing the rest of the crew is on the advanced track as well?" Zinnia looked up and down the hall at everyone rushing to their classes.

I nodded. "Yeah."

Ophelia chuckled. "No pressure or anything."

"Yeah, no pressure." Zinnia sighed.

CHAPTER 19

First Tuck and now my exams. Shouldn't I get a pass from schoolwork or something? How was I going to be ready in two weeks? As we walked down the hallway toward the courtyard, Ophelia flanked me on one side and Nova on the other. It was a crisp mid-October day, and the sky was covered in gray puffy clouds. Cool gusts of wind blew across the courtyard and through my shirt. The moment my boots hit the grassy courtyard, heat hit my skin, and not the kind that came from the sun. The kind I got whenever I sat in front of a fire pit. "What's happening?"

Tuck leapt up onto the fountain and stood over the crowd gathered around him. I could see Patty Pinch Face and her followers practically salivating as he smiled and winked at them.

Ophelia tapped my arm. "Isn't that your boyfriend over there surrounded by a mob of girls?"

"He's not my boyfriend," I growled. But he was indeed surrounded by them all. His tousled auburn locks stood out against the gray sky, and drops of water from the fountain gathered in his hair and across his gray shirt. When he reached back and cupped his hand in the top tier of the fountain and splashed his flock of followers, a wide smile spread across his face.

An obnoxious giggle stood out louder than the rest. When I looked closer, Patty's large blond curly hair was a beacon in the crowd. Her pink sweater covered a bright white button-down shirt and a short pink plaid skirt. If only I had the power to make people step on Legos while barefoot for the rest of their lives! Because Patty Pinch Face with her overly preppy outfit and her loud cackle would be my first victim. I curled my hands into fists at my sides.

"Well, if I spent days fighting for some guy's life, he better not be standing there flirting with another bimbo the next day." Ophelia shifted from one foot to the other. "Want me to get rid of her?"

She took a step toward the fountain, but I reached out and pulled her back to my side. "You can't just go around killing people because you don't like what they're doing." As much as I wanted to let her go and punish Patty for hitting on Tuck, I knew I couldn't. Though it was tempting.

Ophelia shrugged from under my grasp. "I'm not going to kill her. I'm not a monster, you know? I was just going to, I don't know, soak her with water or send a few bees to sting her so she'd have to leave."

Nova chuckled and nodded. "I wouldn't mind seeing that."

Just as I was about to let her loose, Tucker held his hand up and launched three fireballs into the air that exploded into the shape of a T. The girls around him clapped and giggled. He flipped off the side of the fountain, then sucked in a deep breath and blew fire from between his lips. Heat warmed my face, and students all around the courtyard stopped and stared at him.

Ophelia leaned in closer to me. "Your boy is a bit of a show-off."

"He usually isn't." Something was wrong with Tuck. I knew him, and this was not him. Tuck liked to keep a low profile, do his job, and get out. Jumping around throwing fireballs was not him at all. I marched up to Tucker and the girls surrounding him. "Tuck?"

He reached into the fountain once more splashed water over his face and hair, then laughed as Patty swatted at his arm playfully. When he turned to look at me, his eyes were as black as night. The smile dropped from his face. "Zinnia."

I stepped in closer to him, and I could feel his body heat pouring off of him. His warm, woodsy scent invaded my nose, and I sucked in a deep breath. "Are you okay?"

He ran his hand over his face, then stared down at me. His eyes shifted from black to honey. He looked around at the crowd and down at himself. "Am I okay? Um, yeah." He shook his head. "I think so."

I lowered my voice. "Then what are you doing?"

His brow furrowed. "I was just, having some fun?"

Patty pushed in on his other side and wrapped her hand through his arm. "Yeah, we were just having fun." She waved me away. "Run along."

"Isn't there like an Izod or polo convention you need to be getting to?" Nova tilted her head with attitude. "So maybe *you* should run along."

Patty's eyes locked on Ophelia, and she pursed her lips. "Who are you?"

"None of your business," Ophelia snapped back, then turned toward me. "I'm going to class. I'll catch you later."

Before she could step away, Patty squeaked. "Oh my God, I know who you are. So, the rumors are true. Zinnia has brought a traitor into our school. Go figure."

Tucker's fingers slid into my hand. No one else noticed, and for a moment I couldn't believe he would do it around so many people. When I looked up into those honey eyes, he smiled down at me and whispered, "Can we get out of here now?"

I squeezed his hand and tugged him closer to me. "You're soaking wet."

Steam rose up from his body, and his hair fell back into place as though he'd never dumped water on it. The dark water spots on his shirt disappeared, and within seconds he was completely dry. "There, can we go now?"

"Ophelia, come on." Nova wrapped her hand around O's elbow and gave a gentle tug. "She's not worth your time."

Patty shoved her way between Nova and Ophelia. "Tell me something. What's it like living a life where everyone hates you and your family?"

An evil grin spread over Ophelia's face, and Patty withered under her gaze. O titled her head and met Patty's gaze. "What was your last name again? Bower-guard, was it?" Ophelia stepped up nose to nose with her. "Your family has a lot of money and likes to put it in places where it doesn't belong. You think you're spilling my secrets by telling people I'm Alataris' daughter? News flash: everyone knows that already. But what they don't know is what your daddy has been up to. Shall I share with the class, or will you be the one moving along?"

"Bitch." Patty's lips turned down, and her face pinched into a scowl.

Ophelia hauled her arm across her body and let it fly. The back of her hand cracked across Patty's cheek, sending Patty straight onto her ass. Patty's pale skin turned a bright angry red, and her eyes filled with unshed tears. Her flock of followers, the girl with an oversized forehead and the other with stringy faded blond hair, squatted down beside her and grabbed her arms to haul her up off the ground.

All around, other students covered their mouths, laughing. Some even started a low chant of "fight, fight, fight."

Ophelia popped her hip and looked down her pert little nose at Patty. "Who's the bitch witch now?"

I moved to go grab Ophelia when Tuck tugged me back to his side. I shook my head. "But Ophelia—"

"Can clearly handle herself." He tugged my arm, and this time I let him take me.

Nova shooed me away. "Go ahead. I got this." She grabbed O's elbow and pulled her away from the crowd. "Let's get to class, Rocky."

"Who's Rocky?" O wrinkled her nose at the name.

I didn't want to see how the rest of that convo went.

I just drifted along at Tuck's side as he led me away. "How are you feeling?"

He dropped my hand and shoved his fingers into his pockets. "Better, thanks to you and Ophelia."

The warmth from his touch seeped from my skin, and I wanted to reach out and take his hand back in mine, but I didn't. We didn't need any rumors swarming around us right now. Not when I just got him back. "I know, Ophelia of all people. It's crazy. But, Tuck, that wasn't you out there. You've never acted like that before."

"I was just having a little fun, you know. Blowing off some steam." He shrugged and shoved open the door to the training center.

I arched my eyebrow at him. "Literally."

The door closed behind us, and we were alone for the first time since we'd been on the island. The training room was what every high school gym I'd ever been to looked like, plus an array of swords, whips, knives, throwing stars, staffs, and pretty much any weapon I could think of lining the walls. Blue mats covered the floors. At one side of the room ropes hung down from the ceiling, along with punching bags and dummies made to take a beating. The distinct smell of sweat and bleach stung my nose. Outside, the hallways bustled with activity, but in here the sound was muted by the doors. Sunlight shined in from the windows around the top half of the room. Tuck had yet to turn the florescent lights on, so the room was dimly lit and quiet, giving us a moment of peace . . . alone.

Tuck turned to face me. His eyes flashed from honey to black and back again. He took slow steps toward me. His gaze was laser-focused like a lion on the hunt and I was caught in his sights. I swallowed and took a step back. My back pressed into the wall, and I had no place to go. My heart raced so fast I could hear my pulse racing. Every time his eyes flashed black, I didn't know what to expect. Would the hex make itself known? Was it a side effect from the potion? It worried me to see him like that. But when the honey color shinned through, I knew he was with me. No hex would hold us back from each other. The future was uncertain, but I had this moment with him, alone. And I was going to take it.

He stalked toward me, looking delicious in that gray shirt and dark jeans. He brushed his auburn hair back from his face, and my eyes were locked on his plump lips.

Tuck reached out and took a lock of my hair between his thumb and pointer, and he wound it around his finger. His lips were a breath away from mine. "On the island when Alataris . . ." His eyes flashed black. "When he hexed me, I thought you'd be killed."

"I wasn't. I'm here and you're here. That's all that matters now." I reached up and brushed my hand over the side of his face. "Are you sure you're okay? Your eyes, they're changing."

"What do you mean changing?" He held his breath and blew it out. "Ophelia said the hex would present itself in odd ways. Do you think that's what it is?"

"I'm not sure." The truth was it scared me to see those honey eyes disappear. What did it all mean? And who could we trust to tell? If Niche or Matteaus found out they'd lock him in a room somewhere and study him. I couldn't be away from him, not now, not again. Worry like I'd never known flooded my body and all I wanted was to wrap my arms around him and make sure he was okay. "But I'm scared."

He pressed his other hand to the side of my neck and ran his thumb over my skin in a sensual rhythmic motion. I closed my eyes, reveling in the feel of his warm touch on my skin, his woodsy smell surrounding me and how close his body was to mine. It was only a few days ago that I thought I would never have this with him again. My hands fisted his shirt, and I found myself pulling him in closer to me.

"Zinnia." He whispered my name like a prayer. "Thank you for saving my life."

When I looked back up at him, his eyes shifted to a

warm honey that melted me from the inside out. "You would've done it for me."

He nodded and moved in closer. His lips pressed into mine, and an electric shock whizzed through my body. Every ounce of me sparked with life. I wrapped my arms around his waist and pulled his body against mine. The hard planes of his chest pressed into mine, and the warmth from him seeped into me. His lips opened, and I let my tongue dance with his. A low growl rumbled in his chest, and he grew impossibly warmer. I clutched him harder to me. I never wanted to let him go.

I pulled back for a second. "Don't ever do that to me again."

His body was flush up against mine. "I promise." He pressed his lips back to mine, and his minty flavor invaded my mouth once more. "Don't put yourself in danger for me again, Zin."

"I can't promise that." I kissed him. "I can't be without you."

He broke our kiss and let his forehead rest against mine. "I know exactly how you feel." His chest heaved with each breath he took. "There's something I've been meaning to tell you since that night on the island."

He reached down and unclipped the clasp on my bracelet, then reached down and pulled his hand free of the cuff he'd worn since the day I'd met him. Then he wound our fingers together and brought the back of my hand to his lips. It was the first time I'd seen his soul mate mark. In my heart I knew we were soul mates through and through. But to have him finally admit it was something I never thought he'd do, not until our fight with Alataris was over. His wrist pressed to mine, and our marks were finally touching. The endless infinity signs moved over my skin, and the pearl-like beads in each one glowed a shining white light. When they touched warmth spread through my chest. The kind of warmth that felt like coming home, like I'd finally found the one place I belonged. Excitement and happiness bloomed, and I couldn't fight the smile on my face. He was mine and he finally admitted it.

After all this time waiting for him to say something, waiting to know for sure it was him, this was soul deep satisfying. In my gut I'd always known it was him. Now we could finally admit it to each other. My heart soared and I felt like I could fly with his wings of fire. My body trembled and I wanted to be closer to him, to lie in a bed and wrap my arms around him for hours on end. I bit my bottom lip. "About time."

He kissed the back of my hand. "You're it for me, Zin. It's always been you since the day we met."

My smile broadened and I must've looked ridiculous. But I didn't care. "Really?"

He nodded. "Really." All too soon he put my bracelet back on and tugged his leather cuff back into place. "But no one is ready for this yet. If Niche finds out or anyone else, they would send me back to Cindalore, back to my home. And I can't let that happen."

I shook my head. He was right. It was forbidden for us to be together. The knights and queens couldn't date at all for fear of it ruining our judgment. Once long ago when another set of knights and queens fought against Alataris they'd almost lost all of Evermore to him. One of the queens had fallen in love with her knight. Alataris exposed this weakness and used it against them, killing every one of them. He saved the couple for last so they could see what their love had done to their friends. Ever since then it'd been forbidden for a knight to love his queen. I wanted to believe Tuck and I were different. No, I knew we were.

I shook my head. "I don't want that to happen either. We are better together. If they send you away—"

"Shh." He pressed his finger over my lips. "So we keep it our secret for now."

I wound my hand in his shirt and tugged him down for another kiss. His lips were firm and soft all at once, and I never wanted it to end. His hands wound in my hair, holding me in place.

I pulled away from him and met his warm gaze. "We keep it our secret."

"In that case…" He leapt ten feet back and pulled a paper out of his back pocket. "I had your schedule changed to help you with your Magtrac exams. There's no way you'll be anything less than advanced once I'm through with you."

I shrugged out of my backpack and let it drop to the floor. "You think so?" I summoned my blades to my hands. The blades themselves were half-moons in my hands, with half circle blades and straight hilt. On one side a phoenix was etched into the metal and on the other side the mark of the queens.

Tuck's lips pulled up in that half-smile I loved. White light burst from the palms of his hands, and the tips of his swords slid out of each of his hands. The metal gleamed with phoenixes etched into each one. He wrapped his hands around the hilts and spun his swords at his sides. "Show me what you've got."

I ran full speed at him. Adrenaline flooded my body, both from our kiss and from the prospect of training one on one with him. His eyes flashed to black, and his smile dropped from his face. He ran at me and held his swords high. He leapt up and brought them down over my head. I held my hands up and blocked his blow with my blades. It was like getting hit with a sledgehammer. I felt the hit vibrate down my blades, into my hand, and burn the muscles in my arms.

I shoved his swords away. "Ouch."

Tuck didn't say a word. He spun on his heels and jabbed his sword forward, catching the tip of his blade on my shirt and putting a little tear in it.

I swung my arm down again, knocking his sword away. "Hey, I like this shirt."

It already had rips in it and I wasn't angry, but he was going too hard. With his other hand, he swung out and I bent backward. The blade missed my cheek by mere inches. "Tuck, stop!"

I ducked around him and came up behind him and kicked out the back of his knee.

He dropped down, sucking in deep breaths. "You're better than I thought."

"Um, thanks?" I held my blades at my sides, ready for his next move. I didn't have to wait long. Tuck propelled himself up from the ground and backflipped over my head and landed behind me. From the corner of my eye I saw him draw his sword back, about to jab it forward. I turned and stumbled away from him. "What's wrong with you? Stabbing me in the back, seriously?"

Again, he said nothing. He moved like a machine set on kill mode. He stalked forward and swung out. I blocked one then the other. I planted my foot and booted him in the chest with the other. He skidded back but didn't fall. He narrowed those black eyes at me and then stepped forward, poised to strike.

Was this his hex? His eyes would turn black and he'd become more aggressive? My fighting skills consisted of flying by the seat of my pants to defend myself. Whereas Tuck had spent his entire life training to be a knight. The blades in my hands shook as I held them up. How would I defend myself against this? *Shit, shit, shit.* "Tucker Brand, stop!"

He staggered back and shook his head. "What happened?"

The training room door flew open and smacked into the walls with a bang. Nova was practically in tears she was laughing so hard. "I can't believe you slapped her."

Ophelia shrugged. "Someone had to."

I kept my eye on Tuck. His breaths heaved in and out of his chest, and he stood there staring at the sword in his hand like he didn't know how it got there. His eyes wavered from black to honey and back again. He pressed the heel of his hand to his eyes and shook his head.

Cross came in right after them. "Yeah, but next time maybe don't make it so public. You could get expelled for that."

"It might be worth it." Nova dropped her bag on the floor next to mine and pulled her hair up.

I clutched my blades harder and waited for his next move. There was a difference between training and being attacked. Sweat soaked my body, my breath heaved, and I couldn't take my eyes off him.

"Are we interrupting something here?" Ophelia strolled out onto the blue mats to stand at my side.

Tucker shook his head and let his swords disappear. Confusion covered his features. "I don't think so."

I threw my blades down, embedding them onto the mats beside my feet. I didn't know what to think. Terror and worry for him overcame me at the same time. I was pretty sure he'd just attacked me. My hands shook at my sides, and I just needed a moment to think. I stomped over to Ophelia and grabbed her hand. "We have to talk now."

"Zinnia, wait," he called out after me.

I couldn't wait. I had to figure out what was wrong with him and I had to figure it out now. "I need to talk to Ophelia. I'll catch up with you later, okay?"

Tucker's shoulders hunched and he looked at the ground. "Um, yeah, okay."

I didn't want to leave him when he clearly needed me, but I had to get to the bottom of this. I pulled Ophelia out into the hallway and glanced around to make sure no one was paying attention to us. I leaned down and whispered, "Something is wrong with him."

"Who?"

"Ugh, Tucker, the guy you helped me save."

She looked up and met my eyes. "Tell me exactly what you saw. Exactly, Zinnia, do not leave anything out."

"We were in the training room . . . alone. And I thought we were going to work on my combat skills for the Magtrac exams. But when we started fighting his eyes, they flashed black. Like pitch-black. It was freaky, and then he attacked me." The words rushed from my mouth. "It's not the first time I've seen them go black either. They keep changing."

Ophelia wrapped her arms around her midsection. "Okay, first, let's not panic."

I shifted from one foot to the other. "I am panicking here. I mean, he was super aggressive."

"Wait a second. Did he attack you or was he just being aggressive during the training? There's a difference."

"Um." I honestly didn't know. I felt attacked, but maybe I was being overly cautious. "I don't know."

"Okay, so let's not leap to extremes. We don't even know what this is yet." She rested her hand on my arm. "But you have to be careful. Watch your ass with him."

"Is it the hex? Be honest with me. I have to know what I'm up against here. I have to know what I need to fight." I wanted her to give me something to do, otherwise I didn't know what to do to aid him. Helpless was something I never wanted to be, especially when it came to Tuck.

O shook her head. "It could be the hex or it could be a side effect from the potion. We need more time to figure it out. I mean, the dude has got a lot of stuff in his system. He's not going to be normal right away."

"I don't think we have time." I curled my hand into a fist. "I'm going to tell Niche."

I went to step by her, but O reached out and pulled me to a stop. "If you do that, they'll lock him in a room somewhere and the hex may never reveal itself. It needs a catalyst. There is a reason it comes out. The only way to find out why is to watch him closely. Then we go to Niche and tell her what we saw so she can help us. But if you go too soon, we may never know. Then what will you do? Keep the pretty bird in its cage forever?"

She was right. If I said anything to anyone, it could end up getting Tuck locked away before we knew exactly what was wrong. There was only one way to find out. Let him go about his daily life and watch him like a hawk. "No, you're right."

"Good." She shoved away from the wall. "Then we keep this quiet. And, Zinnia?"

"Yeah?"

"I'm serious, watch your ass. No more being alone with secret lover boy." She pushed away from the wall and walked back into the training room without another word.

I'm so screwed. The only person I can talk to about this is Ophelia . . . yeah, I'm screwed.

CHAPTER 20

Ophelia's breaths fell into a steady, even rhythm, yet I couldn't sleep. Next door I could hear Tuck moving around his room. He seemed to be as restless as I felt. What happened to him today? Was the hex causing him to be more aggressive, prone to showing off and fighting? Or was it a side effect? I had to know. "Screw it."

I kicked my legs over the side of my bed and padded barefoot to the door. When I turned the knob, it creaked ever so slightly, yet Ophelia's breathing didn't change.

"So, we're still going to pretend that I'm sleeping and you're not sneaking out, right?"

I jumped back from the door and pressed my hand to my chest. "You scared the crap out of me. And yes, we are pretending exactly that."

"I saw something in a movie like this. Big sister sneaks out, little sister covers for her. It was stupid. Here's a tip: don't lock yourself out, and if you get caught, I'm so not covering for you." She pulled the blankets in closer to her face. "Good luck, big sis. And if you're not going to listen to me about not being alone with him them make sure you bring protection."

"Ew, we don't need condoms. We haven't even . . . you know."

She held her hand up. "Stop right there. I meant bring a knife or something in case his eyes go all creepy. I do not want to know what my sister is doing behind closed doors."

I rolled my eyes. "Don't call me that."

"Whatever you say, sis."

When I pulled the door open and peeked out into the hall, it was empty except a few pixies buzzing about. Kumi lay up against the wall across from my door. I froze. *What are you doing here? I thought you went back to your room on the beach.*

Yeah, no. Something doesn't smell right. I'll just be here.

I opened my door a little wider. "You can come inside."

Kumi didn't hesitate. She got up and trotted right past me, pulled the blanket from my bed, threw it on the floor, and planted herself right on top of it.

Make yourself at home . . .

The door creaked again as I pulled it closed behind me, and suddenly, I was nervous to knock on his door and try to talk to him. Not because of what happened today but because I was going into his room, at night, in nothing but my black cami and a pair of too short gray shorts that would fall off if it wasn't for the drawstring. I glanced up and down the hall once more, then raised my hand and knocked on his door. I wrung my fingers together as I waited and listened to him moving closer.

He yanked the door open and his eyes widened in surprise. "Zinnia."

My jaw dropped, and all forms of speech were completely forgotten. Tuck stood before me in nothing but a pair of dark gray sweatpants. Sweatpants that fell so low on his hips I could see every muscle in his stomach and then some. His abs were toned, and as my eyes traveled lower, they tapered off into a perfect V-shape that peeked out over the top of his waistband. *Tan skin . . . so much tan skin.* That wicked phoenix tattoo ran from just under his ear all the way down the side of his neck. My fingers twitched with the need to trace it.

He didn't say anything else. He simply took a step back and held the door open for me. I didn't hesitate to walk in. I spun in a slow circle, taking in every aspect of his room. It was nearly identical to mine, with large dark wooden book shelves, a four-poster bed, and a heavy wooden desk. Two other doors told me there was a bathroom and closet in his room as well. The only difference between our rooms was his was immaculate and mine was, well . . . not.

His door didn't creak as he closed it and flicked the lock into place. He shoved his hands in his pockets and walked past me to sit on the bed. "What are you doing here?"

"I couldn't sleep."

"Oh, no?" He spread his hands out behind him and leaned back a little.

I walked up to him and pressed my leg between his to spread his knees wider. When he let me, I stepped between his thighs. "Look at me."

I ran my finger over his neck and down his jaw, forcing him to lift his gaze to mine. When his smoldering honey eyes danced with little sparks of red, I knew I was with the real Tuck. The one who was my soul mate, the one I fought to save. "What happened to you today?"

"I-I don't know." He turned his head away from me. "I keep losing chunks of time. I remember being someplace one second and the next I was someplace else doing things I don't remember doing. It's not safe for you to be around me, Zin. You shouldn't be here."

Since the day I met him, I wanted to run my fingers through his hair. Now I didn't hold back. I let my hands brush through those auburn locks as I moved in closer to him. "I almost lost you. You can't ask me to be away from you right now. I need to be here to feel you next to me."

He leaned forward and wrapped his hands around the backs of my thighs. His touch was so much warmer than everyone else's. I could feel the roughness of his warrior hands against my skin, and his fingers rose higher and higher. When he looked up at me, I could see the questions in his eyes, could see him hesitate to touch me. But this was Tuck. He was mine and I was his. I wanted him to touch me. I wanted to feel how alive he was after he came so close to death only days ago. I wanted to be around him while his eyes were honey and I knew he was himself.

I leaned down and pressed my lips to his. Strands of his hair tangled within my grip as I moved closer. Tuck dug his fingers into my legs as he lifted me up and brought me back down to straddle his lap. I sucked in a breath and smiled into our kiss. His arms wrapped around me in a tight grip, pulling me closer to him. My chest pressed into his, and I could feel his pounding heart through the thin material of my tank top.

The world titled sideways, and he spun around and

tossed me onto his bed. I fell back, landing in the soft pillows. Tendrils of my hair fanned out over the burgundy sheets. Tuck crawled up my body and settled himself over me. Though we were both still in our clothes, this was the closest we'd ever been, and I wanted it, wanted him more than anything.

He leaned down and brushed his nose against mine. "You are so beautiful."

When he brushed his lips against mine, I let my hands run up his bare back and held him tighter. My nails dug into his skin and pulled him close, wanting to feel him against me. "Is this okay?"

He nodded. "More than okay." His eyes flashed black, and he shook his head.

"What's wrong?" I pressed my hands to the sides of his face, forcing him to meet my eye. "Look at me. You need to stay with me here, Tuck. Fight this."

The onyx melted away, back to his warm honey color. He slumped over and moved to lie beside me. He plucked up a strand of my hair and toyed with it, wrapping it around his fingers. "I want to be with you, Zin. But I have to figure this out first. If something happened to you because of me . . ."

"Nothing is going to happen." I wanted to reassure him, to help him see that nothing, not even a hex, could tear us apart. But even I questioned if it was safe to be around him or not.

He pressed his lips together and nodded. "Yeah, it'll be okay. But for now, why don't you just stay here a little longer, okay?"

I curled onto my side and pulled one of his pillows under my head. Tucker wrapped his body around mine, spooning me. When he wound his arm over my hip, I grabbed his hand and brought it closer to me. His fingers entwined with mine, and we lay like that—for how long, I didn't know. Long enough for his body to go limp against mine and his breaths to grow deep and even. My eyes grew heavy. I let myself drift off, surrounded by his warmth and with his fingers tightly wrapped in mine.

CHAPTER 21

"*The power to bind is the power to hate. Destroy that which you hold as your dearest mate. Forfeit the balance of sanity's mind if hate does not rise and claim her life in three weeks' time. Turn to the hunt and let the games begin. Taking her life is the only way to win.*"

His voice whispered through my mind, low and hissing. With each breath I took, choking smog filled my lungs and burned my body like acid from the inside out. I wanted to push him away, but I was trapped, caught within his clutches. My arms and legs thrashed, and the sense of falling seeped into my stomach. I fought against it with everything in me. A scream tore its way up my throat.

"Tuck! Tuck, wake up!" Someone shook my shoulders so hard my eyes flashed wide open.

I scrambled back up the bed and looked down at myself. Blackness forked out in my veins and ran all over my body. A thick smoke covered my hands, and when I looked up, the room was covered in a haze. "Zinnia? Zin."

I tumbled from the bed and shoved myself up against the wall. That voice whispered in my mind. *Destroy that which you hold as your dearest mate? NEVER!* I drew my sword, ready to fight him off. The curse of trying to kill my Zinnia. The hazy mist slowly lifted from my vision, and my darkened bedroom came into view. I pressed my back to the wall and fought to catch my breath. I ran my hand through my hair only to find it covered in sweat.

Zinnia stood next to my bed with a blanket pulled up to her neck. She held one of her hands out to me. "Tucker? Tucker Brand, are you okay?"

Am I okay? My eyes darted around the room, looking for the voice that beckoned me to hurt her, the man I now hated more than any other in the world. I rubbed at my eyes. "Where is he?"

"Where is who? There's no one here with us." She took a step closer. "It's just you and me."

I shook my head, ready to fight for her, to die for her. "No, he was here. I heard him."

"Tuck, put the sword down. It's just us. You had a nightmare." Zinnia came even closer to me.

Claim her life in three weeks' time. I dropped the sword to the ground like it'd burned my hand. *Claim her life? Never.* I reached out and pulled Zinnia into my arms and pressed my nose to her hair, inhaling her sugary vanilla scent.

When she wound her arms around my waist and hugged me to her, my heart sank. "Don't worry, Tuck. We'll figure this out. It's going to be okay."

How is any of this going to be okay? "I know. It'll all be okay." I would never hurt her, and if I had to go insane to protect her from myself, then so be it. I pressed a kiss to her hair. "You better go before everyone else wakes up. If anyone sees you leaving my room . . ."

"I know." She tipped her head back and pressed her hand to my cheek. "You sure you're okay?"

Not in the least. "Yeah, it was just a nightmare." *Or was it?* "I'll be fine."

Once I figured out how to break this hex and not kill my soul mate, everything would be fine . . . maybe.

CHAPTER 22

I sat on a stool in the middle of the room. Potions class was going to start any second and Zinnia had yet to get here. There were nine other lab tables. Each of them was a long rectangular shape with a heavy cauldron in the middle of it surrounded by vials, flasks, and tubes. A burner sat just beside it. Everyone else's tables were filled with lab partners, and mine had yet to arrive. I tucked a lock of my hair behind my ear and pulled my book out from my backpack.

"Ugh." Zinnia slammed her bag down on the table next to me.

My head snapped up, and I could instantly tell something was wrong. Dark circles hung under her eyes, and her hair was wilder than usual, sticking out in a million different directions. She wore a big baggy hoodie, jeans, and UGGs. An outfit that took zero effort. "What the hell happened to you?"

"I didn't sleep well." She yanked her book and notebook from her bag and slammed them down on the table. People at the tables next to us all turned to look at her. Zinnia froze and glared at them. "What?"

I held my hands up. "Whoa, cool it there, tiger. What's going on?"

Zinnia climbed onto the stool next to mine and leaned in closer to whisper, "Tucker. He's not okay. I mean, we knew the potion would only wake him up so the hex could present itself, but so far I think it's just driving him to the brink of insanity. And things have been happening."

"Wait a second, what kind of things?"

She brushed a lock of hair behind her ear and glanced around the room. "His eyes have flashed black a few times and I think . . ." Her voice cracked. "I think the hex is presenting itself, but we don't know what it is."

I leaned in and turned my head in her direction, making sure no one could see my mouth. "Who's we?"

She groaned. "Ophelia."

"Ophelia? Really? You trust her with this." I began to stand up. "We need to talk to Niche."

Zinnia's hand darted out and she pulled me back down. "No, if we do that what do you think they'll do?"

I peeled her death grip from my forearm. "They'll isolate him from the rest of us to try and keep us safe."

She nodded. "Yes, and if they lock him in a room somewhere, we will never figure out what the hex is. And that means we will never cure him of it. Ophelia said the only way for the hex to be revealed is to let him go about his normal life until it's obvious."

"Unfortunately, that's true. I learned it in my curses class last year." I bit my bottom lip. "But, Zin, this is serious. He could hurt you or someone else."

She shook her head. "I don't think he will, not really."

The other students were still chatting and laughing among each other. It was loud enough so no one could hear us. Even so, I scooted my stool closer to hers and leaned in. "What makes you say that?"

"Last night I was in his room and I—"

"Hold up, what were you doing in his room?" I knew there was something between the two of them. But any kind of relationship between knights and queens was strictly forbidden. It could endanger the whole crew if two of them favored each other over the rest of us. But I knew Tuck and Zinnia would never do that. Even if they loved each other, the crew would come first.

"I was, um, well, I was . . ." The room fell completely silent and the door slammed, drawing my attention away from Zinnia and toward the front.

Ophelia stood just inside the door, wearing black fishnet stockings, a stretchy pink pencil skirt, and a leather jacket that cut off just at her elbows. Her long black hair was wound in a big, puffy bun on the top of her head. The outfit was a far cry from the Wednesday Addams look I'd seen her in when she was working for her father. She glanced round the room, then looked behind her. "What? Is my skirt stuck in the back of my fishnets? Do I have an emergency girl code going on or something?"

When no one answered, she rolled her eyes. "Okay then." She took two steps and made a move to sit at the first available table, but one of the other students placed their books in the spot. Ophelia paused, then moved to the next table where a girl with frizzy red hair dropped her backpack on the chair. "My partner is on their way."

I glanced at Zinnia and could see the concern in her eyes. I shook my head. "No, she has to figure this out on her own."

"It's not like you and I don't know what it's like to be an outsider in a new school. Besides, you keep your friends close and your enemies closer, right?"

Whether or not she meant it, I did indeed know what it was like when it came to being a new girl in a school full of people who already knew each other. It didn't help that we were all considered queens and stood out at a time when everyone in our grade was also trying to stand out. As the Queen of Death, people avoided me. Well, all except Zinnia. I wasn't even too close to Serrina, the Queen of Desires, or Tabi, the Queen of Elements. Sure, we all liked each other and got along, but it wasn't until Zin arrived that I felt I fit in with someone.

I nodded. "Right."

I sighed and pulled my backpack off the seat next to me. "O, over here."

Ophelia's head snapped up, and a small smile spread across her lips. She wound her way through the lab tables and stood before us. "Um, thanks. It's a tough crowd in here."

Patty, who sat in the front of the room, turned around and narrowed her eyes. "Your father either killed or enslaved some of their families. I wouldn't expect a warm welcome. Who knows what kind of blood runs in your veins?"

"Careful, or I'll make sure there's a bruise on your other cheek to match the one I gave you yesterday." She dropped down into the seat next to me and shrugged off Patty like anything the girl said didn't matter. If I wasn't so suspicious of her, I would high-five her. She pulled a pack of chips out of her bag and popped them open, shoving a handful into her mouth. "What'd I miss?"

Zinnia shifted in her seat. "Nothing. That's a cute outfit. I don't recognize any of it."

"Oh, yeah. Some of the other queens gave me the clothes they don't need. Like three garbage bags full. I think the skirt is Tabitha's and the jacket is Serrina's."

"Wow, I'm glad they're pitching in." Zinnia looked at me with wide eyes.

"I might've mentioned to them that we needed some extra clothes for O. She did help Tuck, after all. It was the least we could do." *I still don't trust you.* But I wasn't a complete jerk. I didn't know if I could trust her or not. But if we were nice to her, maybe she'd slip up or hell, even give us some good intel on her father. She didn't seem like she was in a hurry to get back to him. Why was that?

"So, Zin, back to what you were saying."

She waved my comment away. "It's nothing. We can talk about it later."

It wasn't nothing. There was something wrong with Tuck, and I wanted to help her figure it out. But I guess talking about it in class was not a good option. Searching for anything to say, I changed the subject to the task at hand. I turned back to Ophelia. "Professor Davis is kind of a hard-ass in this class. If you need my notes, I'll let you borrow them."

Ophelia pulled a piece of paper from her bag and

unfolded it. She scanned over it, looked up at the clock and back down at the paper again. "This is advanced potions, right?"

"Yeah?"

"I think I'm good." She shoved the paper back into the bottom of her bag.

"If you say so." I handed my notebook to Zinnia. "Here are my notes. I know you'll probably want them for your Magtrac exams."

Zinnia reached out and yanked them toward her. "Yeah, we can't all be as overconfident as O."

"Hello, Queen of Potions and Spells here. It's not overconfidence. It's just a gift." She leaned her elbow on the table and shoved another round of chips into her mouth. The bag rustled, and I swear I could hear each chip crunching in her mouth.

Professor Davis opened the door and closed it quickly behind her. She was a rotund woman who appreciated the ancient ways of the craft, which reflected in her choice of clothing. She wore a thick brown cloak that fell from her shoulders down to the floor. Tuffs of her frizzy salt and pepper hair stuck out in all different directions. Her chubby cheeks held a rosy undertone, and when she smiled, her whole face lit up. "Now then, where were we?"

Patty raised her hand and waved it back and forth.

"We were about to start a transformation potion." She turned around and stuck her tongue out at O, then turned back to the professor. "You gave us a list of ingredients to use yesterday. Today we were going to make it."

"Ah, yes, right then. Open your books to page 319. You'll find a list of things there and specific directions. Now, I must warn you to follow the directions precisely or the spell will go awry, and we don't want that, now do we?"

Ophelia looked down at her book and raised her hand. Professor Davis folded her hands in front of her and sucked in a deep breath. "Yes, Ophelia."

"I was wondering, what is your opinion on switching the sandalwood oil with dragon scale oil?"

The professor's eyes danced with excitement. "You know, I've heard it gives the potion user at least eight more hours before the transformation wears off, though I haven't tested it out myself. Why do you ask?"

"Well, I actually found that it gives you about ten more hours, and it will change your voice to match whatever or whoever you're transforming into." Ophelia pointed at her book. "See here where it says *add three drops of sandalwood*? I usually add like five of dragon scale oil."

Professor Davis moved over to our table and peered

down at Ophelia's book. "Fascinating. Were there any known side effects?"

"Oh, come on. You can't be seriously taking advice from *her*. She's a criminal." Patty tossed her curly blond hair over her shoulder. "I think we should stick to the textbook."

"And I think you should stick to minding your own business. If another student has something influential to share with the class, then I suggest we take it into consideration." Professor Davis leaned over Ophelia's book. "Have you used it?"

I scoffed. "Oh, yeah. I've seen it."

The entire class all turned and stared at me. I shrank down in my seat. "What I mean to say is . . ."

"What she means is they caught me after I used this potion," Ophelia clarified.

"Well, then it must not have worked very well." Patty chuckled, and like the good little followers that they were, her two little minions laughed as well.

Zinnia scoffed. "We caught her by accident. We didn't know it was her. Trust me." She titled her head to the side, and a questioning look overcame her features. "Why were you in disguise?"

"Um." O glanced around at everyone staring at her. "That's a secret for another time."

I'd been asking myself that same question for a long

time. How was it that we ended up catching Ophelia? Was it a lucky break or a plan to get a man behind enemy lines? There were so many different things going wrong I couldn't help but wonder if she was part of it all.

CHAPTER 23

Three hours later and I had a thorough knowledge of how to transform myself into someone else. Thorough and overwhelming. At any second my brain was going to explode from information overload, not to mention my constant worry about Tuck. I wanted to talk to Nova about it more. Hell, I wanted to call Elle, my best friend from childhood, but how did one say, "So I'm worried about my phoenix soul mate being hexed and losing his damn mind?" It wasn't a normal conversation to have. But I needed advice on it all, my hexed soul mate, my half-sister who couldn't be trusted, my ever-growing power, my exams, my kidnapped mother, and my life-or-death fight against my father. Even thinking about it now was all just too much.

Ophelia practically sprinted for the door the

moment class was over, and Nova had to get to her next class on the other side of campus. I'd been a sophomore in school for all of two months and this was my third schedule. When I looked down at it, I noticed there was a free period for me to take a break. *Thank God.* I needed a second to think to myself, and there was only one place I could think of that I wanted to go. Back to the beach I'd first met Kumi on. That classroom was somewhere near the courtyard. I opened it once and I knew I could open it again. She'd been held within its enchanted walls on a beautiful beach. I wanted to go there and soak up the sun and think it all out. With that in mind, I turned down the hall, ready to find her and lie in the warm sun for just a few minutes. Out of the corner of my eye, I saw a set of strong hands reach out and grab Ophelia, then yank her behind a corner. I pulled my bag tighter on my shoulder and ran toward where I saw her disappear.

Before I could turn the corner, I heard her snap, "What the hell, Cross? What do you want?"

"What are you doing here, O? I thought we agreed I'd go and you'd stay."

I peeked around the corner and spotted Ophelia with her back to the wall and Cross with one hand pressed to the wall next to her head. He leaned in so close that anyone else who would see them would think they were a couple. Cross' dark hair fell over his gold eyes as he leaned in closer to Ophelia.

She pressed her hand to his stomach and then wound her fingers in his long-sleeved burgundy shirt. "No, you agreed. And I could ask you the same question. What have you been up to?"

A cocky half smile tugged at the corner of his mouth. "We both know your father wanted a man on the inside. Or was it a woman?"

"And we both know your father wanted it to be you." When she glanced in my direction, I ducked back behind the corner and waited for them to start talking again.

Cross chuckled. "Maybe I'm here for my own reasons that have nothing to do with my father." I leaned around the corner once more to watch the two of them. They were so close, so familiar.

"Oh, please, and you know I could say the same exact thing." She smiled up at him. "Round and round we go, where this stops, we both will never know. To trust or not to trust you."

"That is the game we always play, isn't it?"

"It's been a game I've been playing all my life." Her voice sounded low and almost sad.

Other students passed by them, staring at two kids of the deadliest men known in Evermore. And they seemed to know each other all too well. It wasn't a coincidence they both showed up. I knew it now, but what did they want with us?

His tongue darted over his lips. "You aren't going to tell me, are you?"

"No. But I'll listen if you tell me why you're here."

"Not a chance, sweet pea." He sighed. "So, what's up with this hex?"

I wanted to run around the corner and demand to know exactly what they knew about it. But if I did, they'd shut right up. It was better for me to remain hidden.

Ophelia shook her head. "I don't know, but I can see there's something up with that guy. I have an idea of what it could be, but I can't say anything until I'm completely sure. No one trusts me as it is."

"Not even her?" He ran his hand down her forearm for a brief second.

Ophelia shook her head. "She's being nice enough, but the big sis is reluctant to let me in. I can't force it. It has to come naturally. But you need to do me a favor."

Holy crap, he knows who I am. Why keep it a secret if he knew?

When I'd first met Cross, I thought he was a cool, distant player, but the way he looked at Ophelia spoke volumes. Were they together? Maybe. Did they trust each other? Only part-time, it seemed. Yet here he was looking at her as if she were the only thing tethering him to this world. "Anything."

"You need to keep an eye on him and keep him away from Zinnia." She reached behind herself and pulled a flyer off the wall and handed it to him. "Especially tomorrow night."

He looked down at the crumpled paper and chuckled. "The school dance. Oh, come on. You want me to be a chaperone?"

Ophelia arched her eyebrow at him. "If that's what it takes."

"I don't know what's involved in a school dance. I've never even been to one. Have you?"

"I've spent my life locked in a fortress. How would I know? Just make sure they stay apart, okay?"

He reached up and brushed his thumb down her cheek. "Maybe you want to go with me?"

Ophelia shook her head. "Not a chance, lover boy. Don't forget I've seen what girls look like once you're done with them."

He turned his head away, and the muscle in his jaw flexed as he ground his teeth. "That was in the past. Before you."

"And I'm sure that line worked on the girls before me." She went up on her tiptoes and pressed a kiss to his cheek. "Just make sure he stays away from Zin, okay?"

He nodded. "Okay."

"Good." She took a step away from him. "I have to go to class."

Cross wrapped his hand around her wrist and tugged her back. "There are no other girls, O."

"Sure, there aren't." She gently pulled free from him and blew him a kiss over her shoulder.

Before she spotted me, I turned away and walked in the opposite direction. I was sure of three things. One, Ophelia and Cross were playing a dangerous game, but whose side were they on? Two, Tucker's hex was getting worse. And three, I needed a date and damn dress for the stupid dance I forgot about.

CHAPTER 24

"Hey, Zinnia. Where are you going?" Nova chased behind me, and her footsteps quickened at she got closer.

She placed her hand on my shoulder, stopping me. I spun around, feeling completely out of control. Everything was coming at me from every angle. I sucked in a deep breath. "I'm leaving."

"What do you mean you're leaving?" We stood at the front gate to the school. The double doors were a thick metal with an oversized lock in the middle of them.

"I'm going shopping. I'm done going on quests, fighting spells and evil kings. For just one hour I want to be a normal teenager and look for a dress for a stupid dance. And then I'll come back and do all that, but just for an hour I need to not think."

Nova nodded. "I know what you mean, and if it were any other day, I'd say let's go, but we can't today."

I stomped my foot. "Why not?"

"It's Alataris. He's been spotted around the city. No one is sure what he's doing, but Niche sent me to find you and make sure you report for your scheduled training. She doesn't want us to engage him until we figure out what he's up to."

"Of course, of course he ruins yet another aspect of my life." I spun on my heels and began marching toward the training room. The courtyard was buzzing with students setting up for the dance. Lights were being hung in long strands, and a dance floor was going down in pieces in front of the fountain. The pixies that flew overhead were buzzing more than usual. They hovered around my head and buzzed around my body. Their tiny whispers were barely discernable, but I did hear two names: Tucker and Patty.

Nova's eyes widened, and we hurried toward the training center. My heart raced as I hurried toward the double doors. When I got to the doors, Nova threw them open and I marched into the center. There in the corner stood Tuck. He leaned up against the wall, smiling and laughing. So different than the Tuck I saw last night, the one who asked me to help him figure out what happened to him. No, this Tucker was carefree.

Patty Bowerguard stood in front of him, bouncing and giggling. At his side, Cross too was carefree and chuckling as though the two of them had some kind of hidden secret joke I wasn't a part of.

I strolled up to them and put on my best smile. "What's so funny?"

"Nothing really." Tuck peered over at Cross and elbowed him playfully. "Right?"

Cross titled his head back against the wall and looked down at me with those glowing gold eyes. "Patty and Tuck are going to the dance together, isn't that right?"

Tuck nodded and smiled. When his onyx eyes met mine, I knew my Tuck wasn't in there. This had to be the hex. Why else would he take a vile girl like her? I knew he wasn't himself, but I couldn't help from feeling a little hurt and possibly jealous.

Patty cackled and sneered at me. "I'm looking forward to it. Are you going with anyone, Zinnia, or are you flying solo?" When I didn't answer, she pursed her lips and tsked. "Aww, you don't have a date. How sad for you."

If I had been Ophelia, I would've cracked her across her face. But I wasn't Ophelia. I was me, and I would maintain control . . . for now. I reached out and tugged at Tuck's sleeve. "Can I talk to you for a sec?"

"Um, yeah, sure." He moved away from the wall ever so sluggishly, and when he turned to face me, it looked like he was stifling the urge to roll his eyes.

This isn't Tuck, it's some a-hole form of Tuck. Who I didn't like very much at the moment. But most of all I was worried. This wasn't him. He would never do this to me. But what could I say to anyone? "Tuck isn't okay because he won't take me to the dance." It sounded as stupid in my head as it would out loud.

On the other side of the training room, the others started to file in. Tabi grabbed up her long golden whip and began practicing with it. The cracking of it echoed off the gym walls. Grayson ran from one end of the training room to the other. His vampire speed sent a light breeze through the room that ruffled my hair. Though Nova was close by, I could tell even while swinging a sword she was listening.

"What's up?" His voice was so casual, so unfeeling.

"What's up? That's what you have to say to me? Why are you going to the dance with Patty? If anything, I thought we would go together." I shifted from one foot to the other, feeling uncomfortable even talking about this. I hoped that seeing me and talking to me would snap him out of it and make him stop being this alternate version of himself.

A dark chuckle played on his lips. "We can do

something else some other time." He lowered his voice. "Or any time you feel like sneaking into my room again."

Black eyes or not, my temper snapped. Did the hex give him free rein to be a complete dick? *No!* I hauled my hand back and smacked him with everything I felt, the frustration of being stuck in the school, of not knowing who to trust, and most of all wanting to trust my soul mate and not being able to. "Snap out of it!"

When Tucker's head snapped back, his eyes had turned back to warm honey. The palm of my hand stung with the force of the hit, and before I shed any tears of frustration I shook my hand out and looked him dead in the eye. "Back to normal?"

He nodded. "I think so." He ran his hand over his cheek where my handprint was outlined in an angry red. "Thanks?"

"My pleasure." Everyone was watching us, and I knew it. I whispered, "We need to figure out what's wrong with you as soon as possible."

He glanced over his shoulder at Patty. "Tell me about it. Did I just agree to go to the dance with her?"

I stifled the need to gag. "Ugh, yeah."

"I'll break that off now."

He moved to step in her direction and I pressed my hand to his stomach. "No, you agreed to it, everyone knows. Just go with her so we don't draw any more attention to us."

He shook his head. "I don't know about this, Zin."

"Just don't kiss her, okay?"

He pressed his lips into a hard line. "You have my word."

"Good, now I'm going to get ready for this stupid thing and then we are going to figure out what the hell is happening." I glanced around at our crew. "It's time to pool our resources and get some help. Becks and Gray can help us."

He nodded. "Agreed, after the dance we stop whatever this is. Until then we keep quiet."

"Deal." I spun around and walked out of the room. I felt their eyes on me. I knew every one of the crew was watching my every move, but I didn't care. I threw my shoulders back and held my head up. I could stomach this for a few more hours. What could go wrong?

CHAPTER 25

I stood before my standing mirror, turning in all different directions to look at the dress I'd found in the back of my closet. It was cute enough, a simple dark purple baby doll dress with spaghetti string straps and a pastel purple bow just under the bustline. I pulled my combat boots on and finger combed my hair. I shrugged at myself in the mirror. "Guess this is as good as it's going to get."

Ophelia leaned in beside me and smiled. "You look great."

"Don't lie. I wore this dress last year to my best friend's sweet sixteen. It kind of makes me look like a little kid." I pinched the hem of the dress and let it drop back into place. Last year I'd been a completely different person. Someone who backed away from uncomfortable situations. Now I faced everything head-on. "I just wanted to be more, I don't know . . . more me? This is so basic."

"It is kind of BB." Ophelia fluffed up her hot pink tutu. I had no idea how she found the things she did, but she was in full-blown eighties glam, with black stockings, a hot pink tutu, a black silky tank top, and the same leather jacket she'd worn earlier in the day. She was pulling my flat iron through her hair, making big curls.

"BB?" I bit my lip and shifted around, looking at how the back felt so plain, so boring.

She placed the flat iron on the table. Then took a tube of lipstick and painted on the dark ruby color. She blew a kiss at herself in the mirror then fluffed out her hair. "You know, basic bi—"

"Don't finish that sentence." I moved toward the closet. "I get it. I'll change."

"Into what? The dance has already started. I can hear the music." She nodded toward the door. "Come on, who cares what you're wearing? Let's just go."

I kicked my boots off. "Just go ahead. I'll meet you there."

"Fine, but you better hurry up. I'm not going to cling to Nova the whole night. It's my first dance *ever*, and I want to enjoy it." Ophelia gave a little wave, then walked out the door.

I stood in my closet, staring at the rows and rows of black clothing I kept and not one dress that would catch Tuck's eye. If I was being honest, deep down I wanted to look my best so he would remember who he belonged with and wouldn't fall to his hex again. But I just wasn't the dress type of girl. There was a light knock at the door, and I left my closet completely frustrated. *How could I have nothing?* "Did you forget your key, O?"

I reached out and pulled the door open and took a small step back. "Cross, hi." I looked back over my shoulder. "Ophelia already left for the dance."

Cross was a stunning guy with his dark hair falling to his jaw and into his golden eyes. He had a strong chiseled jawline and overly full lips. He wore a navy button-down shirt with the first three buttons wide-open, his standard leather pants, and biker boots. "I'm not here for Ophelia."

"You're not?" I leaned up against the doorframe, blocking him from coming in. "And here I was thinking you guys were a thing."

His tongue darted out over his lips. "What gave you that impression?"

I was so tired of keeping secrets and tired of dancing around people to try and figure them out. If he was my enemy, let the chips fall where they may. "I saw the two of you talking yesterday."

"And?" He shrugged.

"And I know you're both here for purposes that are your own. Neither of you trusts the other, and I think because Ophelia asked you to keep him away from me that *you* are the reason Tuck is taking Patty Pinch Face to the dance. Have I left anything out?" I crossed my arms over my chest.

Cross rubbed his hand over his stubbly jawline. "Things with O are complicated right now."

I threw my hands up. "What about the rest of it?"

He held his hands out in front of him in a surrender motion. "Look, I'm not here to hurt anyone, if that's what you're worried about."

"Then why are you here?"

He sighed and glanced down the hallway. "To take you to the Solstice Ball."

I shifted from one foot to the other. "But I don't trust you."

"It's a good thing you don't need to trust me to dance with me." He offered me his hand.

This would be the first ball I'd been to where I had a date. He wasn't the one I truly wanted to be with, but he was gorgeous, and it could be fun. At least if I showed up with Cross people wouldn't be looking at my crappy dress.

I slid my hand into his. "Okay."

"But first, is that what you're going to wear? It doesn't seem like you." He made a show of looking me up and down.

"No, I hate this dress. But stupid Alataris is hanging around the city and no one knows why. So, I couldn't go get a new one."

A deep chuckle vibrated in his chest. "Oh, Zinnia, just because your dad is being a dick doesn't mean you're stuck."

I opened my mouth to yell he wasn't my dad, but Cross chuckled and shook his head. "Your secret is safe with me. Some of us know what it's like to have a father we aren't proud of."

"If you say anything to anyone, I swear I'll . . . well, I don't know what I'll do, but it'll suck for you." I jabbed my finger in his chest.

"I have no doubt it will." He lifted his hand and spun me in a circle. "Now about that dress, what's the point of having all this power if you're not going to use it for fun once in a while?"

"I have no idea what you're talking about."

Crimson mist rose from the palm of his hand, and a

wicked smile played on his lips. "Just hold very, very still."

I took a small step back into my room and he followed me in. The door clicked shut behind him and my heart raced up into my throat. My eyes went wide. "Cross?"

CHAPTER 26

NOVA

Somehow, a canopy of trees sprouted up over the past few hours, covering the whole courtyard like a perfect tent. The branches all wound together, and multicolored fall leaves decorated each of them. Twinkle lights slowly flickered like stars in the night sky. Mason jars hung from the branches, and pixies fluttered from one to the other, lighting them up. The fountain poured in a soft rhythm. Couples swayed back and forth on the dance floor to Ed Sheeran's "Perfect". Tables were scattered all around the courtyard, and a long buffet table stood packed full of all different kinds of food.

At the table farthest from everything sat Matteaus and members of the Fallen. Incredibly, there were eight of them. I'd only seen three of them and now here they were. Each of them draped over chairs that didn't hold their too big bodies. An array of weapons was strapped all over Matteaus. It was the first time I'd seen him carry his legendary dual swords, and I wasn't the only one to notice. Every student who passed by their table stared. They were beautiful to look at, beautiful and deadly, each one with wings blacker than the next. Even the other professors and Niche were there, sitting around the table with them. Which meant no one was paying attention to us.

Grayson held a silver chalice to his lips and took a deep sip. "Bloody good stuff that is."

"Thanks, you look nice too." I flattened my hands over my dress and smoothed out the silver satin material.

"Don't be put out. You know you look amazing." Grayson winked down at me. "I was glad you decided to come with me."

Serrina sashayed up to us. The girl was movie-star beautiful with her long streaked blond hair, pouty red lips, and skin-tight black dress. The dress hugged every inch of her from the thin straps all the way down to just above her knees. "Has anyone seen Brax? He's supposed to be my date."

I shook my head. "He's really been MIA lately." I poked Grayson in the side. "What's up with him?"

"What? What do you mean? I don't know anything." Grayson started to turn away and head back toward the buffet.

"Freeze." I pinched his suit jacket and pulled him back toward me. "That does not sound like you know nothing. Fess up."

"On pain of death, I will not." He took another deep drink, and when he dropped the glass from his mouth, a hint of thick red liquid was left on his lips.

"Oh, for the love of Pete." Serrina held her palm up to her mouth and blew across it. Red magic seeped from her fingers and blew straight into Grayson's face.

He sucked in a deep breath, and the magic drifted up his nose. He swayed on his feet and tried to shake it off.

Tabi moved in next to Serrina and laughed. "Oh, make him dance like a chicken."

She threw her head back and started laughing. Her wild curls fanned out from her face in all directions, and the shining yellow of her dress gave her mocha skin a warm, sunny look I envied. Bright beads were sewn into the halter strap around her neck and across the bodice.

Serrina held her hand up. "Just a second. Grayson, where is Brax?"

Grayson's eyes went heavy-lidded. "In his room."

"Why is he in his room?" Serrina blew another round of magic into his face.

"He's got himself a puppy and he's obsessed."

"Aww, he's always wanted one." I leaned in and whispered, "But isn't that against the rules?"

Grayson nodded sleepily. "Indeed."

Serrina shrugged. "I guess I can forgive him for ditching me for that."

Tabi put her hands on her hips. "Speak for yourself. Beckett just straight up disappeared, and I have no idea where he went. Adrienne is obsessed with getting better at magic and won't leave the library, and Ashryn has decided—and I quote—'I do not wish to attend this event.' More than half our crew is missing." She popped her hip and sighed. "Someone needs to explain to them all that once in a while we need to sit back and enjoy life. Also, I can't believe Tuck is here with Patty Pinch Face. She's a bitch with a capital B. What has gotten into that guy? And where the hell is Zinnia?"

"She's coming. She was changing when I left her." Ophelia strolled up and slid in next to me.

Tabi and Serrina grew silent at her arrival. Even now, it was hard for me to get used to having her in the school, let alone talking to the rest of us. Ophelia had always been our fallen queen, the one on Alataris' side, and now I didn't know whose side she was on. Only time would tell, but did we have the time to wait? The prophecy had said it would take all five queens to stop

Alataris. We started with one man down and now she was back? Or was she playing both sides of the fence?

Ophelia swayed to the music. "Yeah, this isn't awkward at all."

When she turned to walk away, I placed my hand on her arm. "Wait, don't go." I looked at the others, then back at her. "You look good. Must've been hard to pull all those together from what we gave you."

"Actually, it was so much fun. I've never had clothes like this before." She snapped her mouth shut and pressed her lips together like she'd just spilled a secret. "What I mean is, um, well, you know I only had those gray dresses I used to wear. Kind of like a uniform my dad picked for me."

Here I was thinking I had it tough. My heart sank for her. No one else said anything, and I wanted to make her feel comfortable with us. "Well, I like it a lot."

"Thanks."

The music dropped to another slow dance, and everyone seemed to stop and stare at the middle of the dance floor. "Oh . . . my . . . God."

Cross moved out to the middle of the dance floor, looking hot as ever in his leather pants and button-down shirt, but he was not who everyone was staring at. Zinnia was at his side and beaming in a strapless heavily gold-beaded leotard that matched the gold in Cross' eyes. The sweetheart neckline dipped low enough to draw the eyes of a lot of guys at this dance. A burgundy sheer skirt fell from her waist all the way to the floor with a slit in the side that showed off her legs. Long strands of her hair were piled on top of her head in an alluring crown of waves. Gray smoky eyeshadow surrounded her baby blue eyes, making them sparkle like stars in the night sky. Cross wrapped one hand around her waist and pulled her in close to his body, and with the other he held her hand up and started to slow dance with her.

A streak of auburn hair rushed past me, and I leapt into action, grabbing on to one of Tuck's arms. Ophelia leapt in front of him and pressed her hands to his chest. "What do you think you're doing?"

The muscle in his jaw ticked. "Cutting in."

I pulled him back. "Oh, no, you're not. You made your decision to go with Patty. You don't get to cut in after the way you acted."

Tucker shoved a hand through his hair and kept his eyes locked on them. "Yeah, but I didn't mean to . . . Shit, I don't remember."

Ophelia's jaw dropped. "Wait, what? What don't you remember, Tuck?"

He turned and began pacing, all the while watching

Cross with Zinnia. "Nothing. Forget that I said anything."

"No, it's not nothing." She snapped her fingers in front of his face. "You need to tell us."

"Oh, Tuckerrrr." Patty's high-pitched voice stopped us from talking. When she moved in beside him, she walked her fingers up his arm. "Don't you want to dance with me?"

"Ugh, yeah, sure." He grabbed her hand and practically dragged her out onto the floor. All the while, he watched Zinnia, who didn't look at him one time. Not even when he tried to get closer to her.

CHAPTER 27

"Don't you dare look at him." Cross bent low and whispered in my ear.

"I won't look at him if you stop staring at Ophelia." I followed his steps around the dance floor.

He pushed me away from his body, spun me, and then pulled me back in. My dress fanned out around my legs, then fell back to the floor. The bodice was almost corset-like and cut across my legs like a bathing suit. I could feel Tuck's eyes on me like two flames that warmed my skin, yet I didn't turn toward him. If staring at me was what it took for him to hold off the effects of the hex then let him stare.

Cross sighed. "She's kind of hard to miss."

"What is up with you two anyway?" It was good to

know that Tuck and I weren't the only ones who had a difficult relationship.

"It's complicated." The song blended into another, and around the dance floor we went.

"Isn't everything?" Just then, I looked up and my eyes met Tucker's. The honey color swirled in his eyes, and tiny embers smoldered out around them. At that second, I wished I were in his arms instead of Cross'. I knew Tuck wasn't himself, but seeing him here with Patty was a personal kind of torture. Living as a queen in Evermore was an overwhelming responsibility with so many secrets. Even now I wanted Tuck. All of our adventures were a rollercoaster ride of emotions I didn't want to get on. Such high highs and painful lows. I couldn't decide which was worse, having to hide what we were to each other or watching this hex ruin what little peace we had between us. He tried to deny everything between us for so long. And when he finally admitted it all we were faced with more obstacles to overcome.

"Can I cut in?" Ophelia stood before us. She narrowed her eyes at Cross and pursed her lips.

I dropped his hand and stepped away from him. "Of course."

"Thanks." It was the first time I'd seen Ophelia give me a dirty look since we got to Evermore Academy. *I know the feeling.* Yes, I knew exactly what if felt like to see your crush with someone else . . . it wasn't a good feeling.

I glanced over my shoulder in time to see her push him ever so slightly and hiss, "What are you doing?"

I didn't hang back and listen to what they had to say. Lovers' quarrels weren't my thing. By the time I made it over to the punch bowl, Tucker was hot on my heels. If I wasn't so worried about the hex, this might've been a fun night. The music was amazing, and the twinkle lights in the canopy of fall leaves and fluttering pixie made it seem even more magical.

Beside the punch bowl were three girls. One stood in the middle with her hands behind her head. She wore a classic princess dress complete with off-the-shoulder straps and big poofy bottom. "Come on, guys, this isn't funny."

The one on her right, a shorter plump girl with her hair pulled into a tight bun at the base of her neck, pointed at the white dress and gave an evil grin. "Make it pink."

Boom! The dress flashed to a hot pink.

Then the girl on her left, one who wore a princess dress but with a shorter skirt, laughed. "Make it blue."

"Guys, this isn't Disney. Give it a rest." The girl in the center pointed to herself and closed her eyes. "Make it what I want it to be."

The dress turned from a cute baby blue to a Queen of Hearts red with black lace embellishments all over it. The other two hunched over into fits of laughter. The shorter one held her stomach. "That's badass. Okay, you win."

That right there was how magic school should be, fun messing around with our gifts. Not spending every day fighting against an evil king who wanted to take over all supernaturals. Part of me hated how selfish that sounded, and the other part of me knew it was what I was born for. If I wasn't so troubled by everything else, I might've enjoyed my first magical ball.

Once I made it to the punch bowl, Tuck came up beside me. "Can we talk?"

I picked up a cup and ladled some fruit punch into it. "Hi, Tuck. How are you? You look nice. Oh, you like my dress? Why, thank you."

"Come on, Zin. We have to be serious." He reached out to touch my arm, but I gave him a warning look and he dropped his hand.

"I know we do." I motioned to the beautiful atmosphere. "But we agreed, go to the dance then be serious. You need a break, and so do I. Hexes be damned!" I took a sip and fought not to spit the too sweet drink out on the floor. I pressed my hand to my mouth, then put the drink down on the table.

"Look, I don't. I just don't . . ." He stabbed his hands through those wild auburn locks, and in that moment, I remembered what they felt like under my touch. The muscle in his jaw ticked as he ground his teeth together.

I searched his warm honey eyes for what he was trying to say. "You don't what?"

"I don't remember saying anything, okay? I don't even remember asking Patty to the dance. I'm worried. The last thing I remember is you hitting me. Nice swing, by the way. But before that, there's nothing." He looked out over the other couples on the dance floor. "You have to know I want to be out there with you . . . and only you. But this thing inside of me, I have to get it out . . . now."

"Oh God, Tuck. I didn't know it was that bad." I wanted to reach out and run my hand over his cheek, to soothe away the worry around his lips and eyes.

He leaned in closer to me. "Zinnia, I think I'm losing my mind." He pressed his hands to his temples. "I keep hearing this voice and this chant in my head over and over again. It's all I hear. I get no peace from it, even in my sleep."

"No." I shook my head. "You're not going crazy. It has to be the hex Alataris put on you."

The music switched again, this time a dance song that was deafening. I could feel the bass beating against my chest. Ophelia stormed off the dance floor with Cross following close behind her. Patty spun in a circle, surrounded by her followers, when her eyes stopped on Tuck and me.

Tuck ran his finger down my forearm, leaving a trail of heat across my skin. "Can we go somewhere and talk? I just want a minute alone with you."

Patty began stomping over to us, and I turned back toward Tuck. "Okay, let's go."

That cocky half-smile spread across his face, and he grabbed my hand and pulled me down the hallway closest to us. I gathered the bottom of my dress and ran at his side. The hallways were dim and empty. My boots echoed off the old stone floors with each step I took. I felt like we were two celebrities running from the paparazzi.

"Tuckerrrr!" Patty's voice carried down the hallway.

He tugged me closer to him. "Go, go, go." A giggle escaped my lips, and I ran faster. We turned the corner and came to a dead end. "Come on in here."

Tucker pushed the double doors wide-open and pulled me through. Then he grabbed a sword from the wall and shoved it through the door handles. He backed away from the door with his breaths heaving.

Outside the door, I heard Patty's voice, "Come on, I think they went this way."

"The training room again." I strolled around while catching my breath. Not a single light was on. I could only make out Tucker because of the moonlight streaming in from the windows at the top of the room.

Tucker turned around and pressed his finger across my lips. "Shh, don't say a word."

My shoulders shook with the effort to hold back my laughter. Once the footsteps trailed away, Tuck dropped his finger from my lips. "I can't believe I got looped into going with her."

I rolled my eyes. "Neither can I."

"I mean, she's the worst." He shook his head. "I'm so sorry, Zin."

"I know you are. I just hate seeing you with her. Once we figure this out no more Patty for you." I knew it wasn't Tuck. I knew it was the hex.

"I can relate." He took a step toward me.

I took a small step back. "Oh, can you?" Excitement thrummed through me, and I wanted to jump into his arms or make him chase me.

He arched an eyebrow. "Have you seen yourself in that dress?"

"Yes?" I fluttered the soft burgundy material. Cool air brushed over my legs and arms.

"You're stunning." His eyes trailed down my body. "And the boots are perfect."

Again, he was hunting me in the room, following each of my movements. I stepped, he stepped. Then my back was pressed against the wall at the far end of the room where not even the moonlight could touch us. He came so close his chest pressed into me and his warm, woodsy scent clung to the air. Electricity crackled between us, and I felt breathless as he leaned in and let his lips hover just over my mouth.

"Help me figure this out. Help me stop whatever is happening. I couldn't bear it if I hurt you." He lifted his hand and pinched a lock of my hair, then toyed with it between his fingers. "And if I do . . . crack me across the face like you did before."

"I didn't mean to—"

"Shh, if you hit me, I probably deserved it." He leaned in and pressed his lips to mine, and pleasure shot through my body like an explosion. I threw my arms around his neck and pulled him closer to me. His hands ran down my sides, and I hooked my leg around his hip, holding him in place. When his scorching touch pressed into my thigh, a moan escaped my chest. He tasted of minty freshness, and I couldn't get enough of him. Heat came off him in waves and sank into me. I pulled him as close as he could get.

He broke our kiss. "Zinnia, I lo—" He stumbled back

and pressed the heel of his hand to his eye. When he looked up, he swayed on his feet. "No, not again."

I took a step toward him. "What is it?"

"No." He held his hand out, stopping me. "Don't come any closer." He hunched over and pressed both his hands to the sides of his head. His mouth dropped open, and a pained bellow broke free of him. His body shook from head to toe, and he stumbled away from me until he held himself up on the other wall. With his back to me, he placed both hands on the wall in front of himself and took deep, calm breaths. Then finally, he straightened his stance and rolled his shoulders.

My heart hammered in my chest, and my hands shook. "Tuck, are you okay?"

Bright white light exploded from his palms, and his swords were held firm in his hands. "Oh yeah, baby. I'm more than okay."

His voice sounded so off, so wrong. My stomach fluttered with panic. "Look at me."

"With pleasure." He spun on his heels and titled his head down and met my gaze. His eyes were two swirling orbs of blackness. Wings of fire popped from his back and singed his shirt clean off his body. The phoenix tattoo on his neck glowed molten red, and Tuck's head twitched to the side as though in pain.

"Tuck, you don't want to do this." I held my hand

behind my back and summoned my blade. The cool grip appeared in the palm of my hand. I'd never been scared of him before, but seeing him like this made me pity our enemies and worry for my safety.

His wings pumped, and Tuck hovered a few feet off the ground. "Don't I? Destroy that which you hold as your dearest mate." He held his sword high over his head and swooped down toward me, ready to take my head.

I ducked down low, barely dodging the edge of his swords. When I spun around to face him, he'd already landed and stood still as a statue facing me. "Tuck, please don't."

His eyes were fully black, and his face was a mask of cold indifference. His hand struck out and he connected with the center of my chest. My body flew back and smacked into the wall. As I slid down and found my footing, I sucked in deep, gagging breaths. He sprinted forward, swinging his sword so fast I lost track of it until it was pressed to the side of my neck. He leaned in, his voice was a deep growl, not the smooth one I was used to. "Don't what?"

He drew his sword across the side of my neck. Pain exploded through my body as he took a deep slice of my skin. Warm liquid ran down my collarbone and across my chest. Tears of pain spilled from the side of my eyes and a coppery scent filled the air. *Blood, my blood.* If I didn't stop him, he would kill me. I kicked my foot forward as hard as I could, connecting square with his crotch.

He hunched over and I smacked one of my blades into the sword he held at my throat. I spun to the side, thinking I could get away when he dropped his sword and wrapped his hand round my neck and shoved me back against the wall.

"Destroy." He squeezed his fingers even harder and I couldn't catch a breath.

I choked out, "Stop, Tuck. Please."

His eyes flashed honey for a mere second, but in that second, he loosened his grip. I sucked in a breath, and his eyes turned black once more. "Stop with your witch-craft. Tucker is gone and he's never coming back."

"He can and he will!" I swung my blade up and cut a gash in his forearm.

"No!" He swung me to the side like a rag doll then pulled his elbow back and launched me to the other side of the room.

My body smacked to the ground so hard I felt dizzy. Black dots swarmed my vision and I wanted nothing more than to curl in a ball and let him have me. But I didn't. I crawled to my feet and faced off against him. I held my blades up the way the real Tuck taught me. Not this hexed villain.

His shoulders vibrated with laughter. "You think you'll defeat me." He held his arms out wide and every muscle in his body rippled and the wings on his back flared brighter.

I shook my head. "No, but I'll make it damn painful for as long as I can."

He spat on the floor. "I look forward to it."

I waved him forward. "Bring it, bitch."

Grayson held me close and spun me in maddening circles. I threw my head back and laughed. My hair came out of the pins holding it up. "You're making me dizzy."

"Fabulous, isn't it?" He slowed down just enough for me to get my bearings.

"I'm so glad we came together. I'm having a good time." Over the past few weeks, I'd never felt happier. Sure, all five queens had risen, Alataris was going crazy, and my world was turned upside down. But now I had real friends, people I could count on. Becoming a queen had made my family send me away. I'd been alone the whole time. Until Zinnia arrived, yes, it'd been turbulent, but she brought us closer together whether she realized it or not.

"As I am, love. But don't go falling for me. I'm not the sort of vampire to bring a good little witch into my crazy world. And don't even get me started on the curse over my family at the House of Shade. Complete nightmare." He held his arm up and guided me to spin under it.

"Wait, what curse?"

"Nova!" Ophelia rushed onto the dance floor and grabbed my hand out of Grayson's. She was trembling from head to toe, her skin was paler than normal, and her eyes were wide with worry. "Have you seen Zinnia?"

I peered over my shoulder. "No. Why?"

Beckett ran up to Grayson's other side. "Tucker is missing too."

"I wouldn't worry about that lot. They're made for each other. I knew they'd work it out eventually." Grayson shrugged and smiled.

Ophelia squeezed my hand so hard I could feel my fingers going numb. "That's my point. They can't be alone together, not now. Not until he's better. If something happens . . ."

I pulled my fingers from hers and grabbed on to both of her shoulders. "Slow down. What do you mean?"

She wavered from head to toe, and her eyes darted around the whole courtyard. "I think I know what the hex is. I've seen my father use it only one other time before. I wasn't sure, but I am now—"

"Hey, guys. Have any of you seen Tuck? One minute I was dancing with Zinnia and the next they were both gone." Cross ran his hand over the back of his head. "It was so weird."

I narrowed my eyes at him. "Shut up." When I turned back to Ophelia, I shook her hard. "Spit it out. What's happening?"

She swallowed hard and looked up at me with unshed tears in her eyes. "He's going to kill her."

It was like a bomb when off, and I stood frozen on the spot, not knowing what to say or do. Tuck and Zin were our leaders. They made decisions. I shook my head. No, I had to step up. I had to help my friends. "Grayson, go get Brax and start searching the shifter wing. Beckett, Cross, go to the vamps." I cupped my hands around my mouth and called out for Serrina and Tabi. The moment they came over, I started talking. "You two need to check the library and release Kumi. She'll know how to find Zinnia. O and I will check the gym and training room."

Serrina looked from Ophelia at me and back again. "Why, what's going on?"

"Tuck is going to kill Zinnia. Move now!"

We scattered to the wind, hoping to get to them in

time.

I STOPPED JUST outside the training room with Ophelia at my side. Inside, I could hear the clanging of metal on metal. Grayson sped to my side, and Brax was only a few feet behind him.

Gray shook his head. "No sign of them."

Ophelia canted her head to the side. "How'd you get here so quick?"

"Vampire, love." He looked at the double doors to the training room. "What's happening?"

"They're in there." I planted one foot and kicked at the door with the other. It gave only a few inches, then popped back into place. "Something's blocking it."

"I got this." Brax pressed his arm to my shoulder and moved me aside. His body grew impossibly bigger, and tiger stripes covered his arms and neck. Huge tiger fangs hung down past his bottom lip. He took three steps back, then ran full force at the door, then leapt forward and threw his shoulder into it. The door shattered into pieces, sending wooden shards in all different directions.

Smoke billowed out the open door, and fire burned up the walls of the room and on pieces of the floor.

Ophelia and I charged in after Brax. I choked back a cough and tried to see through the darkness around the room. "Zinnia?"

"Over here!" She fell into a coughing fit, and I tried to follow the sound of her voice.

The wind kicked up and blew me back five feet. Ophelia grabbed on my hand and pulled me to the ground. "Look out!"

I flattened myself a second before Tuck swooped right over my head. His eyes were pitch-black, and his lips were turned down into a scowl. His brows were drawn low over his eyes. Sweat and soot covered his face and hair. I didn't think Tuck would ever lose the noble look I'd grown so used to him having, but this . . . this was the face of an avenging evil. "Destroy that which you hold as your dearest mate!"

Ophelia rolled to the side. "He's crazed. We have to stop him before he does it."

I rolled to the side and sprinted toward Zinnia. Tucker swooped down at me once more, and I slid down to the ground next to her. "We have to get you out of here."

Zinnia clutched my hand and crouched even lower. Dust and dirt covered her from head to toe, and she held her blades tight in her hands. The bottom half of her dress was ripped into tatters. Sweat ran down her face, and she scrambled even lower. Blood dripped from a nasty cut on her neck and bruises marred her skin as if someone had strangled her. "It's not Tuck. I know it's not. The hex has ahold of him."

I nodded. "I know."

Tucker landed just in front of us, his wings fully extended out to his sides. "Come out, come out wherever you are, my love." His voice was deep, menacing, not his own.

A loud growl sounded a second before Brax jumped in front of Tuck, hauled his fist back, and connected right with his jaw. Tuck flew backward and landed flat on his back, then skidded across the floor. Grayson jumped up and landed with both feet on Tuck's chest. "Sorry about this, mate." He too hauled his fist back and started punching Tuck. "Just." Hit. "Stay." Whack. "Down." Punch.

A fireball exploded out of Tuck's chest, sending Grayson shooting like a rocket up toward the ceiling. He crashed into it then fell back down to the ground. Cinderblocks rained down on top of Grayson, pinning him to the floor. Tuck rose to his feet like a possessed doll and wiped the blood from his lip across the back of his arm. I pulled my gloves from my hands and let my magic gather on my fingertips.

Beside me, Zinnia let silver tendrils of her magic

seep down her arms. "I'm ready. On the count of three."

I nodded. "One."

Brax charged at Tuck in his full tiger form, tackling him to the ground. Tuck swung out with his elbow, catching Brax in the side of his head. Fire boomed from his fist, and Brax soared across the room and slammed into the wall. He slowly morphed from tiger back to man as he slid down the wall. His cat-like green eyes rolled into the back of his head, and he fell into a heap on the floor.

Ophelia rushed to my side. "Are we gonna do this or what?"

"On the count of three." I nodded. "Two."

"What happened to one?" Black smoke billowed from her hand across the floor.

"Three!" I screamed, and we all ran at Tuck at the same time.

He spread his legs apart, and I fired my magic into the ground, willing the dead to rise up and take ahold of him. Skeleton arms exploded from the ground and wound around his ankles and feet. No matter where I was, when I called the dead, they answered, even if I wasn't on a burial ground. He was rooted in place. Ophelia grabbed a staff from the floor and launched it at him. Tuck swung his sword up, slicing it in midair before it reached him.

Zinnia skidded to his side, and tears streamed down her face. "I'm sorry about this."

Silver magic wrapped around his whole body, and he bellowed to the ceiling. Flames flowed over every inch of his skin and into those silver streams. It was as if his shifter magic was lighting hers on fire or using it to get back to her. I waved my hand, and the skeletons holding him down shifted to try and knock him off balance.

"Zinnia, drop your magic . . . or he'll burn you."

"Ow!" She waved her hand back and forth as if she'd put her fingers on a hot stove. The magic she had surrounding him in fizzed away, and Tuck slashed out with his sword, chopping the skeletons limb from limb. He spun on his heels and headed straight for her like a machine.

Ophelia ran up and jumped on his back, wrapping his head in a sleeper hold. "Stop or I will kill you."

Zinnia hunched over, holding her burned hand in the other. "No, don't kill him. He doesn't know what he's doing."

Tuck reached up and grabbed Ophelia's arm. He spun around and tossed her right at me. She tumbled in midair and slammed into my body, knocking the wind from my lungs. Black dots swarmed my vision, and I tried to sit up. Ophelia lay on top of me, pinning me to the floor.

Tuck chuckled. "Who's asleep now?" He held his sword high and took a step in Zinnia's direction.

Cross and Beckett charged into the room. Blue orbs floated around Beckett's fingers.

Crimson smoke poured from Cross. He shot Beckett a look. "Only you can stop this."

Tucker was only mere feet from Zinnia. He held his sword to her throat. "Destroy that which you hold as your dearest mate."

Blue fog spread across the floor and up the walls of the training area. *Fog? Smoke? He's a warlock.* Beckett hovered up off the ground, blue light shining from his eyes. "Stop!"

The command was instant, and Tucker froze, unable to move. Every muscle in his body tensed to strike, yet the sword didn't budge. My eyes widened. I'd always thought Beckett was a witch, a practitioner of white magic. But this, the smoky magic seeping from his body, the power to control another's will, it was dark magic, powerful dark magic. Beckett expanded his hand, and everyone in the room floated up off the floor, suspended.

Ophelia was removed from my body, and I felt weightless like I could fly. Blue fog covered everything, putting out every single fire. Beckett raised his hand up over his head, and it all gathered like a tornado around

Tuck, holding him prisoner.

When my feet touched down on the ground, I rushed to Zinnia's side. "Are you okay?"

"I think so." She was shaken, of that I was sure. She wavered on her feet, yet she faced Tucker head-on.

Tucker struggled against Beckett's hold. "I will have her. I will carry it out." The magic was so thick around his body that I could only see the top of his head and nothing more. He struggled and thrashed.

Zinnia opened her hands and silver sparkling magic unfurled and mixed with Beckett's magic. Zinnia closed her eyes and sucked in a deep breath. "Moon above shine bright and take his mind to the middle of the night. Relax your mind and let your body flow free until the moment you're locked away safely."

The hex on him couldn't fight both Tucker's inner strength and Beckett's black magic mixed with Zinnia's spell. Tuck's head slumped to the side, and his body went limp.

Becket spun his hands in a circle, and his magic seeped back toward him.

A large smile spread on Cross' face, and he clapped Beckett on the shoulder. "Good job."

"Good job?" Beckett marched over to where Tuck lay motionless on the ground. "Is this why you came to

Evermore Academy, to force my hand? For my warlock side to come out?"

"I don't know what you're so pissed off about. You saved them all." Cross motioned to the charred room, Grayson and Brax lying unconscious and O, Zinnia, and I standing in utter shock.

"Sometimes the end doesn't justify the means." Beck stomped toward the door. "You know where the jail is. Lock him up." Beckett left the room angrier than I'd ever seen him before.

Beckett a warlock? What the hell?

Cross turned back toward the three of us. "I seriously have no idea where the dungeon is in this place."

Ophelia walked over to Tuck and squatted down beside him. "I know where it is. I'll help you get him there."

Zinnia dropped down onto the ground and sat cross-legged, watching with wide eyes.

I sat down next to her. "Are you okay?" I wanted to reach out and hug her, but my gloves were in the corner of the room somewhere and I didn't want to see any part of her future. So I sat with my hands folded in my lap.

Tears spilled down her cheeks. Her hair was a mess, her dress was in tatters, and she was covered in black soot. She shook her head. "No, I'm really not."

CHAPTER 29

Tuck attacked me, but he hadn't hurt me, not really. What was a cut and a few bruises between eternal soul mates? That wasn't Tucker. The Tucker I knew would never hurt me. I was shocked. My body was shaking from head to toe, and I couldn't get it to stop. Cross and Ophelia labored under Tucker's unconscious weight. They each had one of his arms draped around their shoulders, and when they finally dragged him into the cell, they placed him on the floor flat on his back. He only wore black pants and his combat boots. His chest was bare and covered in soot. Sweat dripped from him, and though his eyes were closed, he shivered there on the cold stones.

Cross held his hand out to Ophelia. "Come on, we

should get you to the infirmary to have a look at that bump on your head."

She shook her head. "I have to talk to Zinnia."

I wanted to hear everything she said, but I was only focused on Tuck. I watched the steady rise and fall of his chest. It soothed me in a way I couldn't describe. "I'll just be a minute. I need to talk to Nova . . . alone."

Cross stepped out of the cell with Ophelia's hand in his. With his other hand, he slid the door shut. The metal bars clinked and rattled as he slammed it shut and locked it. "He'll be out for about another half hour or so."

"How do you know?" Nova's gaze never left Tuck.

Cross shrugged. "Because I've seen this magic at work before." Without another word, he pulled Ophelia out of the room and I was left alone with Nova. I wanted to harden my heart against the pain I was feeling. I wanted to think logically, not emotionally.

But this was Tuck, and logic would never dictate how I could act when it came to him. Tears fell from my eyes in rapid succession, and I didn't even try to stop them. My throat felt thick, and I couldn't swallow it down. "Nova, I'm going to ask you to do something for me, and I know it's not right, but I have to prepare myself."

"Please don't ask me." She turned to look at me, and

in that look, she pleaded for me not to ask this, but I had to.

I unfastened the bracelet around my wrist and held the mark out to her. Nova sucked in a shocked breath, and I pulled my arm back in. When I tried to fasten the clip of my bracelet, my hand shook so hard I nearly dropped it. "I have to know." I swallowed down a sob. "I have to know if I need to prepare myself. Is he going to die, Nova?"

She took a small step toward the bars. "I don't want to see."

"Normally, I would never ask, but this time . . ." I moved closer to the cell and opened the door. As I stepped inside, she followed me in and knelt beside him. One by one she plucked the fingertips of her gloves off, then slid the whole thing from her hand. She held her palm over his bare chest.

"Zin, I can't." Her voice wavered, and I knew I was pushing her too hard, but this was Tuck, and if I only had hours left with him, I wanted to be ready.

I dropped down on my knees beside her and placed my hand over hers. Then slowly I lowered her palm onto his chest. Nova sucked in a shocked breath and scrambled back on her hands away from him. Panicked breaths huffed in and out of her chest.

I crawled up next to her. "What did you see?"

247

Nova snatched her glove from the floor and shoved her hand back into it. "He's not going to die." I let out a sigh of relief, and then she looked away from me. "You are."

CHAPTER 30

TUCK

The haziness around my eyes dissipated ever so slowly, letting the world come into view, though there wasn't much to see. My whole body felt like it'd been put through the wringer. My face was tender, and when I reached up and pressed my fingers to my eye, I stifled a wince. With my other hand, I patted the cold ground. Dirt and stone scrapped my palm. As I sat up, a sharp pain shot through my rib cage. I tiled my head back and looked around at the three thick stone walls and set of bars containing me. I groaned. "Where am I?"

"You're in the dungeon of Evermore Academy. Now answer me this. Are you, you?"

I tilted to the side, and every bone in my body felt like it was broken and mended back together like the first time I shifted into my phoenix form. Beckett sat on a bench outside the cell hunched over with his elbows on his knees and his hands folded under his chin. There was no smile on his face. Instead, his ocean-blue eyes were grave and serious.

I gingerly rose to my feet and hobbled over to the bars. "It's me. Tuck."

"Good." He made no move to release me.

I wrapped my hand around the bar and leaned my body up against them. "What happened?"

Beckett sat back against the wall, then kicked his legs out in front of him. "Before or after you attacked all of us?"

"Wait, I did what?" I shook my head. "No, there's no way I could've attacked you guys."

"Tell that to Brax and Grayson. They're both in the infirmary with concussions." He sighed.

"You're joking. This is some kind of mistake." It had to be. I would never in a million years hurt my friends, my fellow knights, in the fight against Alataris.

Beckett shook his head. "I wish it were, my man. Whatever hex is inside you is dangerous, and we were lucky this time. Next time we might not be."

Alataris did this to me. There was no way I would ever hurt any of our crew. They were my friends and damn near the closest thing I had to a family. Mine had let me go long ago and forced me into this life. But now that I had it, I didn't ever want to let it go. I didn't want to let any of them go. "Then keep me in here."

"My friend, I couldn't let you out even if I wanted to. The simple fact is you're not safe to be around." Beckett looked up at me with desolation in his eyes. "Until we figure out exactly what this hex is, you have to be contained from now on."

What if they never figured it out? What if they sent me away from here, away from Zinnia? *Zinnia!*

The last thing I remembered was being in the training room with Zinnia. Her sweet taste on my lips, her warm vanilla scent invading my nose, her soft skin under my touch. She was everything to me. One second we'd been dressed up for the Solstice Ball. Now I was shirtless and trapped in a jail. *Zinnia?* My eyes widened. "Zinnia? Is she hurt?"

Beckett rubbed his thumb over his bottom lip. "Just a couple scrapes and bruises. Nothing serious. I think she's more shaken up than anything."

Scrapes and bruises? I staggered back from the bars and fell onto my ass. "Shaken up? What happened, Beck?"

Beckett sighed and looked down at the floor. "I think it's better if you don't know."

If she had to live through it, then I would bear the knowledge of what I'd done to her. She was my soul mate. What happened to her happened to me. I shook my head, and I could feel the darkness stirring in my chest. "Tell me."

"She was the one you were after. You tried to kill her, Tuck."

I could feel the dark hex rumbling to come out, wanting to take over my body. Before, I hadn't known what it was. Now I knew. But there was something in me that would always be stronger than any black magic living there. The pain of what I'd done to her hit me full force, and I couldn't breathe. My Zinnia, my everything. I'd hurt her. There was nothing anyone could say or do to make me forgive myself.

Flashes of my sword to her neck appeared in my mind. Then like a firing squad, they played one after the other—my sword to her neck, me flying over her and swinging my blade in her direction, her hiding in a smoke-filled room, her desperate coughs as she fought to breathe. Her blood pouring down her neck and coating the tip of my sword. My hand around her neck squeezing the life out of her. They flickered like lightning flashes in my mind. I couldn't see them happening at the time, nor could I stop them. It was as if the hex was showing them to me now just to torture me. It was my job to protect Zinnia, both as a knight and as her soul mate. *I failed.*

I pressed my hands to my temples to try and stop the images from invading me. But they wouldn't stop. I was there. The sounds, the smells, and her terror in each moment were as real as the cell I was sitting in right this second. I rocked back and forth. "Stop, stop, just stop!" I bellowed at the top of my lungs.

Beckett jumped up and ran toward the bars. "Tuck, what is it?"

"Oh God." Pain shot through my head, and I felt like someone had taken an ax to it. I fell onto my back, and my body writhed on the floor as I tried to fight off the visions of Zinnia being hurt.

Beckett banged on the bars. "Tell me how to help you."

You can't. No one can. The phoenix mark on my neck burned hotter than I'd ever felt it before, and I let it. I threw myself over to the fire in my veins, letting it burn me from the soul out toward my skin. My arms turned to wings, my body shrank down, and my face morphed. The pain in my head subsided as I let my phoenix out. I still saw all the things I'd done to Zinnia and the terror I'd rained down on the rest of my friends. I gave one last look at Beckett, then turned from him and moved to the corner of my cell. Here, I was safe. Here, they were safe from me. And here was where I would stay until this hex finally drew the last breath from my lips.

I t'd been a full day since the dance happened and
Nova's prediction about my death. I couldn't wrap
my head around it. I wanted to sit and think about what
she'd told me, but Tuck was in trouble and so were the
rest of my friends. Even now, I marched down the long
corridor toward the dungeons to meet Nova and see
Tuck. Old rectangular stones lined the walls, ceiling, and
floor. Lanterns hung sporadically down the hall, giving
it an eerie, haunted effect. None of the other students
dared to venture down here. Not even the nosey school
pixies would come this way. It smelled of damp earth
and reminded me of a basement in an old house. Kumi
trotted along by my side. In truth, she hadn't left me
since everything happened at the dance.

As if reading my thoughts, her words huffed through

my mind. *I leave you alone for one night and you nearly get yourself killed. If something happens to you, who am I going to talk to? Definitely not your cat friend. Cats are shady. They push stuff off the counter for no reason.*

You won't have to. You can go back to the beach and chillax.

Kumi groaned, and I could picture her rolling her eyes. I reached out and brushed my hand through her midnight fur. It soothed my nerves. I hadn't seen Tuck since I left him unconscious on the floor. Now I was worried seeing me would send him reeling once more. It'd taken time to get cleaned up and explain things to Niche, who even now was buried under a stack of books searching for anything to help him. After Niche and the good doc did a small healing spell on my neck, my wound now looked three days old. Even so it was four inches long and deep. The bruises on my skin turned to dark purple fingerprints that would match Tuck's hand. Not everything could be healed with magic. I wanted to see him, but I stayed away, hoping if he didn't see me, he might miraculously get better.

Ophelia turned the corner and nearly collided with me. She pressed her hand to her chest and jumped back. "A little warning next time, sis. You scared the crap out of me."

"It's not like I was sneaking around." I took a step to the side to go around her.

Ophelia stepped in front of me, blocking my path. "I have to talk to you."

Kumi's lips pulled back from her teeth. *Do we like her? Sometimes.*

Can I bite her?

Not today. I kept on petting her to keep myself from losing my patience.

"Whoa there. Back off, Lassie. I gotta talk to Zin. It's important." Ophelia was the only one of my friends I thought truly wasn't afraid of Kumi. Sure, the others had tried to stand up to her, but they hadn't scolded her with a pointed finger wagging in her face the way O did.

"Can it wait? I'm meeting Nova and we're visiting Tuck." I walked past her.

"I know what the hex is."

My heart went from zero to sixty with that one sentence. I sucked in a breath and turned to face her. "What is it?"

"It's complicated." She moved to stand in front of me and wrapped one of her hands around mine.

"What's happening to him? How do we save him? I can't take much more of this." I pulled my hand free from hers and returned to petting Kumi's side, finding comfort in the rhythm of it.

"Zinnia, there is only one way I know of to save him." She looked down at the ground, and her face paled. She swallowed hard, then looked back up at me. "You have to die."

CHAPTER 32

"How long has he been like that?"

Beckett rubbed at his eyes and yawned. "Since last night."

Tuck sat facing the corner of the cell with his back toward where Beckett and I sat. He was in his full phoenix form with his wings held tight to his body and his head pressed to the wall. Long crimson feathers jutted out from his tail and lay across the floor in a beautiful array of red hues. A small flame burned on the very last feather at the end of his tail. It flickered from red to black and back again. I knew he was struggling to fight against his curse. Every once in a while he'd shudder from head to toe and the flames in his tail would nearly go out. Yet he refused to turn around to face us.

Beckett leaned in closer to me and spoke under his breath. "He hasn't eaten or drunk anything since last night. He just keeps sitting there shuddering in pain."

"What set him off?" I looked at his twitching feathers and listened to the pained grunts he couldn't hold back.

"He asked me if he hurt Zin." Beckett stabbed his hands through his beach blond hair. "And I told him the truth. It's all my fault."

I wrapped my arm around his shoulder. "How could you have known this would happen?"

He shook his head, and the bench creaked under the weight of our movements. "I didn't." He leaned forward and called out to Tuck. "Tuck, come on, man. You have to at least drink something. You can't live like this."

I stared at Tuck's back, reading his soul. The desperation, the pain, and the overwhelming sadness that were within him were suffocating. I squeezed Beckett's shoulder. "That's just it."

Beckett turned his head and met my eye. "What's it?"

"Maybe he doesn't want to live . . ."

CHAPTER 33

ZINNIA

"What do you mean I have to die?" I crossed my arms over my chest and leaned up against one of the walls. Kumi rumbled a low growl. *She's lying. She just wants you dead. The little traitor.*

I want to hear what she has to say. Wait for me back on the beach. I'll be there soon.

No, you need me to stay. Kumi sat like a dog in training, planting herself at my side.

I'm not making any decisions right now, and I need a second to think. I gave her a pat on the shoulder, and she walked away with her nine tails swishing.

"Now back to me dying." Maybe it was true. I was going to die. This was the second person to tell me in two days it was my time to go.

Ophelia shook her head. "No, you don't have to die.

Well, I mean, you kind of do if you want to save Tuck. But only for a little while."

I held my hand up. "That makes no sense at all."

"Look, I've only seen Dad use this hex one other time before, and it really drained him. I didn't think he'd do it to you. But I was so wrong because all the signs are there, and I should've seen it sooner. But I didn't, and I—"

"O, breathe and explain. You're babbling." I grabbed her shoulders and held her still.

"The hex, it's a curse really. Tuck either has to kill you to lift it or . . ." She looked up at me with eyes so wide I could see my own reflection in them.

"Or?" I was hanging on her every word. I had to know exactly what I was up against.

"Or he'll be driven to madness and eventually he will kill himself from it."

I dropped my hands from her shoulders. "Why are you telling me this?"

"Because I have an idea. It's a bad idea but an idea nonetheless." A half smile pulled at her lips, and in that moment, I didn't trust her. Not one bit. Yes, she'd been good for the past few days. But that didn't mean I trusted her with our lives.

I put my hands on my hips. "Tell me your idea."

"Have you ever heard of the potion Sleeping Death?"

I had no clue what she was talking about, but it sounded as dangerous as ever.

I shook my head. "No, never."

"Basically, you drink the potion and it'll give your body the illusion of death."

"The illusion? How would that even work? You can't just pretend to kill me and think the hex will lift. I actually have to be dead." A shiver ran over my body, and I didn't know if it was from the cold dungeon or the fear I felt at the prospect of actually considering this.

Ophelia bit her bottom lip and looked up at me from under her lashes. "Well, you would actually be dead. Technically speaking."

"O, would I die or not? Stop messing around and give me details exactly how this would work." I was only ten feet from Tuck's cell and needed to go see him.

"It would first put you into a sleep-like trance, then your body would cool, and eventually your heart would stop." She stepped to the side to let me pass by. "But it's temporary, and only lasts for ten minutes. Which would be long enough for the hex to leave Tuck's body forever."

I trudged toward the room where his cell was. "How do you know it'll work? I mean, has it ever been done before?"

Ophelia shook her head and held her arm out in front of me, stopping me from turning the corner into where Tuck was being kept. "Look, I get that you don't trust me yet, but I am telling you Tuck doesn't have much longer until he's completely crazed. I've been wracking my brain trying to think of ways to help you, and in theory, this will work and it's the best you've got. I've spent all night in the potions lab with Cross perfecting this."

"Hold up, you already made a potion to hypothetically kill me?" Anger flared in my chest. I hadn't agreed to this, not even close, and she was already trying to kill me.

"Don't look at me like that. I'm just trying to help you." She dropped her arm out of my way. "I'm doing more than anyone else."

"Yeah, plotting to kill me is doing a lot. You and Cross, the two people who just happen to show up at school at the same time all this goes down. The two people who have fathers in very powerful positions across enemy lines—"

Ophelia leaned in and hissed, "Let's not forget who your father is too. That makes you my sister, and I'm sorry, but I don't want to see my sister die or lose her soul mate. If that makes me a bad person, then so be it. At least I have a solution. What have you got?"

I sucked in a shocked breath and whispered, "Who said he was my soul mate?"

"Oh, please, like it isn't obvious." Ophelia rolled her eyes. "You wanted an option, I gave you one. Whether you use it or not is up to you." She waved me past her and into Tuck's cell.

I froze for a moment. What if what she said was true? She wanted to help save her sister, her family? Or was she just that good at playing the innocent friend? I was torn and didn't know which way to go or what to do. All I knew was I had to see Tuck with my own two eyes and make sure he was okay.

I rounded the corner and pushed through the outer door and walked into the room where Tuck's cell stood. In the corner sat Tuck in his phoenix form, his back to us, and he rested his head against the wall. Beckett and Nova jumped to their feet when I walked in.

I motioned to Tuck. "What's this?"

"He's been like this since he woke up yesterday." Beckett looked like total crap. His eyes were glassed over and bloodshot. He pressed his hand to his mouth and stifled a yawn.

I made a move to step closer to the cell, and Beckett's arm shot up, stopping me. "I wouldn't if I were you."

I looked down at his arm and back up at him. Why was everyone treating me with kid gloves? I'd survived worse than a gash and some bruises I'd gotten when taking on Tuck. "What, why not?"

"Because when I told him about what happened, he had a breakdown of sorts." Beckett narrowed his eyes at Nova and shook his head, and Nova pressed her lips together, saying nothing.

I shoved his arm away. "What aren't you guys telling me?"

"He grabbed his head and started screaming and shaking before he exploded into a ball of fire and came out like that." He pointed at Tucker. "He hasn't moved since."

"I can tell he's in pain. Every once in a while, he moans and twitches." Nova shook her head. "I don't know what else we can do for him. It's like he's trapped in his own mind."

I glanced over my shoulder at where Ophelia leaned up against the wall by the door. She didn't look up, just wrapped her arms around herself and shook her head. If I had to choose between Tuck and myself, it would be him all the time. I called out, "Tuck?"

The phoenix's back stiffened, and he turned his head to the side. Though he was in his bird form, I would know those honey eyes anywhere. "Tuck, it's me. Please, please just talk to me."

The phoenix leapt to the side, transforming from

bird to man. In an instant, Tuck stood at the back of his cell. His face crumpled in anguish, and he pressed his hand over his bare stomach. "I'm so sorry I hurt you."

I shook my head and took a step toward the cell. "You didn't hurt me."

He squatted down and wrapped his hands around his knees. "Don't lie to me." He pressed his finger to his temple so hard his arm shook. "I see it here in my mind. Over and over again. I see the cut on your neck and oh God, are those my fingerprints?"

"Look at me. I'm fine." I pulled my collar higher, trying to hide how close he came to killing me.

He rocked back and forth while poking himself in the temple. "I see it. It doesn't stop." He stabbed his hands in his hair and let his head fall onto his knees. He started murmuring to himself, "Destroy that which you hold as your dearest mate." The words flowed out of his mouth until they blended into one long sentence and his eyes went vacant.

"Tuck, stop. I'm here. I'm fine." I moved even closer to the cell bars.

Tuck leapt to his feet and ran at the bars. His body slammed into them at full force, and he smacked his head as he reached out for me. "Come here, come here. Destroy that which you hold as your dearest mate." His words were frantic, like a zombie going for the kill in a horror movie.

A line of blood trickled down from where he hit his forehead. Beckett wound his hand round my arm and yanked me back a few feet. "Maybe you should leave."

"You want me to leave him like this?" I shook my head. "No, I can't."

"What else can we do?" Beckett stepped in front of me and held his hands at the ready. All the while, Tuck rammed his body into the bars again and again, reaching out from me.

Grayson raced into the room and took one look at Tuck and gave a low whistle. "What rabid dog bit his ass?"

"Shut up, Grayson." I turned and faced Ophelia. "I know exactly what we're going to do. O, go get that potion."

CHAPTER 34

"You can't seriously be considering this. Not after I told you what I saw," I said even while I carried one end of a heavy cot out of a cell down the hall from Tuck's and Zinnia carried the other end.

"What choice do I have?" As we turned the corner and shoved the cot through the door, Zinnia remained resolved.

"For starters, Ophelia will kill you the first chance she gets, and right now you are just lining up for it. Like a cow to the slaughter. How do you know this wasn't Alataris' plan the whole time? Come on, think about it. Her showing up here, with the flower and being so cool and so fun. It could all be an act." I slammed the cot down outside Tuck's cell.

"Just so you know, I heard everything you said,"

Ophelia snapped as she walked into the room behind us with a vial of dark purple liquid in her hand. "And for the record, I'm not going to kill her." She looked down at the potion. "Well, not so she stays dead."

"I'm through debating this. Look at him." Zinnia motioned toward Tuck, who paced the cell like a lion in a cage. Every so often he'd smack himself in the head and mutter that line or he'd turn and hiss in Zinnia's direction.

"Well, don't you think we should at least wait for the rest of the crew to be here? I'm sure they'd have something to say about this, don't you?" I was stalling. I knew this was an epically bad idea, but at the same time I could see the logic in it, especially if it actually worked.

"Niche will stop this for sure, and the others will try to as well. I can't risk that happening. So whoever is in this room either stays here for the long haul or you need to leave, because either way this is happening." Zinnia plopped down on the cot and swung her legs up on the end of it. She held her hand out to Ophelia. "Give it to me."

I stepped forward. "Wait, just a second. How is this supposed to work?"

Ophelia handed Zinnia the vial. "Once she drinks it, she'll fall into a death-like sleep. Her breathing will slow and then her heart will stop."

"For how long? I mean, can't she get internal damage from that?" I didn't want Zinnia to do this. I really didn't. And I would try to convince her not to. "It's just so risky."

Ophelia shook her head. "Not really. The magic will protect her organs. In ten minutes, she'll wake up as if nothing ever happened."

"I don't like it." Grayson crouched down by Zinnia's head. "It seems too good to be true. And you know what they say. If it looks like a duck, and quacks like a duck, it's a bloody duck. She could kill you here and now."

Zinnia pulled the top of the cork from the vial. "It's a risk I'm willing to take."

CHAPTER 35

"Beckett, time me."

Grayson rose to his feet and moved to stand beside me. "I can't believe you're going along with this."

"I'm not." I narrowed my eyes at Ophelia. "If this doesn't work, I'll kill you myself. You've seen my power. You know I can do it."

"Relax yourself, Malibu Ken. It's going to work." Ophelia moved to the foot of the cot and patted Zinnia's leg. "I'm here for you."

Zinnia nodded up at her and held the vial to her lips and tipped it back. The purple potion slid down her throat, and Zinnia fell back on the cot and dropped the vial on the ground. It shattered to pieces. I hit the timer on my watch. I kept my eyes locked on her. Her skin paled, and her lips turned a sickly blue. "Is it supposed to work that fast?"

Ophelia's mouth dropped open, and her eyes bugged out of her head. "I-I don't know."

Nova wrapped her hand around Ophelia's upper arm and shook her. "What do you mean you don't know?"

Her head bobbed back and forth on her shoulders. "I mean, how could I know? I've never tested it before."

"Oh, shit." I bent down and grabbed Zinnia's wrist and checked her slowing pulse. Her breaths became slower and slower until the last one whooshed out from between her lips and she grew so still.

Nova dropped O's arm and started pacing. Tears streaked down her face, and she pressed her hand to her mouth. "Oh God, I knew this was a bad idea." A sob broke past her lips, and she shook her head. Her shoulders bounced with each sob that left her. Her tears didn't stop, and she fell to her knees beside Zinnia's bed. Tucker fell like a brick on the floor of his cell. He flopped onto his back and lay there spread out like a starfish.

I looked down at my watch. "Five minutes."

Tucker's veins turned black under his pale skin, and his body convulsed. Beads of black sweat lifted up from his skin, like rain in reverse, until it gathered into a cloud over his chest. His eyes flashed wide-open just as the cloud disappeared.

"Three minutes." My arms shook, and I couldn't take my eyes from Zinnia's too still body.

"Oh God, Zinnia." Tucker jumped to his feet and banged on the bars. "Let me out. Let me out now."

Grayson raced over to the cell and yanked the metal frame open. Tuck rushed out and scrambled to the other side of Zinnia's bed. He gathered her hand in his. "What the hell happened? She's ice-cold."

"She killed herself." Nova sobbed. "For you."

"No, she didn't!" Ophelia stomped her foot. "It's just a spell. She'll wake up any minute now." Her voice wavered, and she didn't sound as confident as she had when this all started.

Tucker's eyes widened, and he wrapped his arms around her shoulder and hugged her to his chest, rocking her limp body. "Wake up, baby. Wake up."

I glance down at my watch. A sheen of nervous sweat covered my body. "Two minutes."

Tucker pulled her closer, and tears poured down his face. "No! No, you can't die. Not now, not when we've gotten so far."

I met Ophelia's panicked gaze. "She better wake up or it's your neck."

"She'll wake. Come on, Zin. My ass is riding on this." Ophelia bounced from one foot to the other.

"Thirty seconds." My throat was thick, and I tried to swallow around it.

Tucker held Zinnia with one arm, and with the other hand he reached up then brushed her wild midnight locks from her pale face. "Don't leave me. Please," he pleaded. "Come on, breathe, Zin. Just a small breath."

I stared down at her still chest, willing it to move, willing her to wake from this fatal mistake. I glanced down at my watch. *Five . . . four . . . three . . .* She didn't move . . . *two* . . . Ophelia betrayed us all . . . *one.* I dropped to my knees.

Nova cried out and fell to the ground, curling in on herself. "I saw this. I saw it."

"Time, Beck?" Tucker didn't look away from Zinnia. "How much longer?"

Tears prickled my eyes, and I couldn't answer him. How could I tell him the girl he loved was never coming back, was never going to smile at him or boss any of us around? I cleared my throat, trying to swallow the ball of emotion and whispered, "Time's up."

Tucker titled his head back and roared as his face crumpled into a mask of grief. Tears fell from his cheeks, dripping into her hair. "Why did you do this for me? Why?" he screamed at Zinnia. He hugged her back to his chest and buried his head in her neck, rocking her gently, all the while whispering, "Wake up, please, God. Please just open your eyes, Zin. Please."

No matter how much he begged and pleaded, Zinnia's eyes didn't open . . .

KEEP the magic alive with *Wicked Potion*! CLICK HERE to order Wicked Potion!

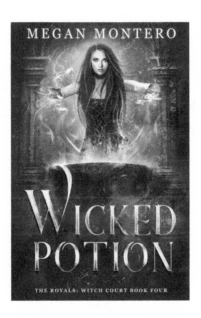

In the war for my power only one will win...
My secrets are starting to surface and in the world of

Evermore secrets can get you killed. The sister I never asked for has joined our side. I've hidden the blood tie we share from everyone, including my soulmate Tucker.

I'm hiding too many things from everyone and I'm starting to unravel.

We don't stand a chance against Alataris, not the way we are right now. His power grows every day. There's only one way to beat him – steal his crown. It's the deadliest mission we've taken yet, and it could get us all killed. But without it we've already lost...

SEE the epic conclusion of Zinnia and Tuck's story in *The Royals: Witch Court Book 5* . To order *Wicked Queen* CLICK HERE!

My power, my reign...

I thought I knew danger, I was wrong. That wicked potion was just the beginning. I feel strong with Tuck by my side, but we're in way over our heads. We need heavenly Fire. It's the only thing that can destroy Alataris' crown. And we can't beat him any other way. That crown is the seat of his power...and I'm going to take it from him.

This is my deadliest mission yet, but I'm out of options and out of time. I have to stop running from him and face my father head on with everything I've got. He thinks he'll win, he thinks I'll buckle after he summons the ultimate evil. But he has no idea what I'd do to protect the people I love. I will take him down, even if I die with him.

This is a family affair and it's time I show my father just how Wicked a Queen can be...

THE MAGIC CONTINUES with *Wicked Omen*! The first book in season two *The Royals: Warlock Court*. To pre-order *Wicked Omen* CLICK HERE.

There's no such thing as magical powers.

Most orphans grow up in foster homes not penthouse suites on the Upper East Side. Everyone always tells me how lucky I am. I know they're right, and I am grateful...but I don't belong here. It all feels so...empty.

In the pit of my stomach I know there has to be more to the world than this. The money, the spoiled rich life doesn't feel like my own. Darkness lingers all around me and I feel it's draw. It sings to me like a siren's song and I've lost the willpower to ignore it.

And then he shows up. His name is Beckett Dust, and he's infuriating. Drop dead gorgeous, but he makes my blood boil. He tells me of a secret world hiding in plain sight, one of magic and power. He paints a pretty picture of a life I'd always dreamed of then takes me to a magical academy to train for a war I have to fight. I'm surrounded by people who want me to fail and he is nowhere to be found.

I'm in over my head and now... they want to use me as a weapon.

For the latest news, events and to get free books join my newsletter simply Click Here!

WANT to connect with me and other fans of Evermore? Click Here to join my reader group on Facebook!

DID you read the prequel novella *Wicked Trials?* Do you want to learn how Tucker and his knights got started? Great News- it's FREE- if you sign up for my newsletter! Click Here to sign up and start getting WICKED with your free ebook now!

THIS POWER CHOSE *ME*...

Within the supernatural world of Evermore everyone prays their child will be born with the Mark of the Guardian for they have unparalleled strength, intelligence, and *power*...but they have no idea what it's actually like. I didn't wish for this *gift* and I definitely don't want it. I was born a prince, I already had it all. This Mark on my neck stole all of it from me and forced me into a dangerous life I'd gladly trade away if I could...

But now the Witch Queens have ascended and it's time to try and defeat the evil King once and for all. For over a thousand years his cruelty has spared no one as his torturous power grows stronger. He must be stopped now, before his reign destroys everything and anything in his way. So I must push aside my dreams of returning home to the family that cast me out. I must step up and claim the power that chose me. I *must* enter the Trials and become a Knight in the Witch's Court.

There's only one way to prevent the tyrannical king from destroying everything I love...I must become the one thing he can't beat.

WANT to see Zinnia's first days in the wicked world of Evermore. Click here to get your copy of *Wicked Witch.*

It's time to claim my power...

All my life I've lived under lock and key, always following the strict rules my mother set for me. A week before my sixteenth birthday I sneak out of my house and discover *why*. Turns out I am not just a normal teenager. I'm a witch blessed with a gift someone wants to steal from me.

And not just anyone...*the* evil King Alataris.

For a thousand years the people of Evermore have suffered under his tyranny. The Mark on my shoulder says I am the Siphon Witch, one of five Witch Queens fated to come together and finally destroy him. The only thing keeping Evermore safe is the Stone that shields the witch kingdoms from Alataris's magic...and now he's found a way to steal it. Suddenly, I'm sent on a quest to find the ancient spell to protect the Stone. My only hope for surviving is through my strikingly beautiful and immensely powerful Guardian, Tucker. The laws of Evermore state that love between us is strictly forbidden, and it appears I'm the only one willing to give in to the attraction...

When the quest turns more dangerous than expected I realize I have absolutely no idea what I'm doing. I was raised *human*. But I have to learn my magic fast because If King Alataris gets his hands on me he'll steal my magic *and* my life...but if he gets his hands on the stone we *all* die.

THE MAGIC CONTINUES in *Wicked Magic*! CLICK HERE to order *Wicked Magic*.

They all fear my power...they should.

FINDING out I'm a witch was a shock. But now that I'm in the world of Evermore I'll do anything to protect it even if that means dying...

The evil King Alataris has stolen my mother, my life, and now he's taken something that could unleash hell on earth. With a powerful Ice Dragon under his every command there is no telling where he will strike next. The Witch Queens have been tasked with saving Evermore. The only problem? The others fear the wild, powerful nature of my magic and sometimes so do I!

The only one who can help me contain it is my protective Knight, Tucker Brand. But even he has his own set of secrets. My feelings for him are overwhelming and strictly forbidden, if we give into the fire we share for even a moment we will lose everything.

When it comes time to take back what Alataris has stolen we set out on our most perilous mission yet. To save the Dragon and Evermore before it's too late. If we fail, the world as we know it will come to an end...and all will be lost for Evermore.

CLICK HERE To order Wicked Magic!

ABOUT THE AUTHOR

Megan Montero was born and raised as sassy Jersey girl. After devouring series like the Immortals After Dark, the Arcana Chronicles, Harry Potter and Mortal Instruments she decided then and there at she would write her own series. When she's not putting pen to paper you can find her cuddled up under a thick blanket (even in the summer) with a book in her hands. When she's not reading or writing you can find her playing with her dogs, watching movies, listening to music or moving the furniture around her house...again. She loves finding magic in all aspects of her life and that's why she writes Urban Fantasy and Paranormal.

Learn about Megan and her books by visiting her website at:

Www.meganmontero.com